FOURSQUARE BOOKS

Also by Nancy Parsons

More From The Better Mousetrap
with Dick Amsterdam

Bald As A Bean: The Experience of Sudden Hair Loss

Abigail's Unicorn

Ye Canna Join In Oor Games
Memories of a Scottish-American Childhood

Brothers of War: The P.O.W. Experience
with James F. Arsenault

The Dog That Managed Hedge Funds

Two-Thirds of a Ghost
A Nell Bane Novel

THE GHOST WORKS A PUZZLE

A Nell Bane Novel

Nancy Parsons

THE GHOST WORKS A PUZZLE
Nancy Parsons

Published by
The Cheshire Press
A Division of The Cheshire Group, Inc.
PO Box 2090
Andover, MA 01810-0037
www.cheshirepress.com

ISBN: 978-0-9853689-9-9
Library of Congress Control Number: 2013954749

Printed in the United States of America

Parsons, Nancy
Two-Thirds Of A Ghost

For Jamie

"She's not a bad woman," Elizabeth said.

"Affairs aren't usually about good and bad," I said.

"What do you think they're about?"

"Need," I said.

Robert B. Parker
The Professional

Chapter 1

"1925," said Nell when the door opened.

"What?"

"1925—the year your house was built. Some people guess weights. I have a passion for architectural sleuthing. I'm Nell Bane."

"1924, actually. Come on in. I'm Angela Shilliday."

The woman opened the door wider by way of invitation. She was uncommonly tall with a body that looked rigorously gym-toned. Dark hair pushed casually back from her face fell in loose waves. Nell, stepping into the foyer, took this in, aware as she did so that Angela Shilliday was conducting a similar once-over.

"I was close on the date though," Nell smiled.

"Close," the woman conceded, "but not accurate. I am a stickler for accuracy."

Then *she* smiled. Nell was reminded of a shark. Although she doubted sharks could smile. Perhaps it was the eyeteeth. But no, that would be a carnivore.

"Touché," Nell said peaceably.

Angela Shilliday gestured into the house. "I thought we'd meet up in my study on the third floor, but since you seem interested in architecture, perhaps you'd like to detour on the way up so you can see some more of the house?"

"I'd like that very much," Nell said frankly. "This house is magnificent."

She did not add that a tour would give her more options for assessing her potential client. People's houses, like their clothing and speech, could be very revealing.

Angela Shilliday proved a brisk tour guide, marching Nell at quite a clip through the living and dining rooms—both capacious spaces with white walls that offset dark beams and woodwork. Nell was dazzled by the elaborate window treatments. Nell, herself, didn't have window treatments. Curtains were what she had in her little Newburyport antique, and very few of those. Those windows that didn't have shutters were bare.

"Porch is off the living room just there." Angela waved toward French doors near a fireplace and hustled Nell past a den and into the kitchen.

Nell was struck by the whiteness—by the wonderfulness of the room—large as a hotel kitchen and outfitted with creamy cabinets, pale gray granite countertops, pristine subway-tiled walls, and—pulled up to the huge island—a fleet of fashionable industrial stools.

"Oh, this is splendid!" Nell breathed. "What an enviable kitchen."

"Do you cook?"

"Yes, I do. Soups are my specialty. I bought a small Aga just to keep soups simmering nicely."

Angela gave Nell a curious look, and in Nell's opinion a slightly distasteful one, as though Nell had just admitted a fondness for scrubbing bathtubs.

"Hmmm."

Then it was back to the front hall with Angela Shilliday rattling off details about the objects and places they passed.

"That's my husband's study."

Nell, peeking into the handsome room left of the foyer, glimpsed another fireplace then she hurried up the wide front staircase to catch up with her quick-stepping guide. But at the landing, she stopped with an exclamation.

"Oh! What a glorious window seat. Perfect for curling up with a book on a rainy day."

"Yes, isn't it." Angela stopped too. "The girls like to play here. They pretend they're traveling on a ship."

"I can understand how they'd love it."

Nell's eyes traveled up to another elaborate window treatment that spanned the upholstered seat cushion. But then they were off again—like following the White Rabbit through Wonderland, Nell thought—and she found herself in the master bedroom where even the king-sized bed seemed dwarfed.

"Terrace off the bedroom," Angela recited before pushing through the master bath and into an adjoining small room with a single bed.

"And this is the snoratorium."

"I beg your pardon. What did you call this?"

"Snoratorium. You know, where you go to sleep when your bed partner starts snoring. Or when one of you is ill."

Nell chuckled.

"It would be embarrassing, though wouldn't it, to wake up in your bed in the morning and find your partner sleeping in the snoratorium?"

They both laughed, and Angela paraded Nell out into the hall and up a flight of backstairs, less grand than the front.

"My office is up here," she said over her shoulder. "High in an aerie where I can work undisturbed. 'Far from the maddening crowd'," she quoted blithely as they climbed.

"Madding," Nell corrected silently. "I, too, am a stickler for accuracy."

But Angela was continuing, "Actually, the family rec room is up here but that's handy, because I can keep an eye on the girls while I work."

She ushered Nell into her third floor office at the front of the house. Windows deep in dormers and shaded protectively by the eaves outside made the room cozy. But Angela had chosen to sit with her back to these windows and had placed her desk chair to face the door, presumably to provide oversight to her children at play. A computer stood ready for business on the desk between slippery columns of papers and manila folders. Two large photographs, handsomely and expensively framed in silver, were positioned to be noticed by visitors. One featured Angela and her husband with their two little girls. In the other, the Shilliday family, with the senior Shillidays centered between their three grown children beamed out into the room.

"That photograph looks like an Elsa Dorfman."

Nell indicated the larger one, and Angela seemed immensely gratified.

"You recognize it!"

"Well," Nell said modestly, "her work is outstanding, isn't it? There are a lot of copycats now but the original always shines through."

Angela lifted the framed photograph carefully and passed it to Nell. Using her manicured pinkie as a pointer—like a big drop of dragon's blood, thought Nell—she introduced her husband's family.

"That's Dad."

Tap-tap-tap on an extraordinarily handsome man in his mid-sixties. His hair had been closely shorn, to minimize encroaching baldness Nell supposed; obviously blonde in an earlier time, his hair shone blonde-white.

"Dr. Thomas Shilliday," Angela explained. "Cardiologist of some note, I might say."

"Distinguished," Nell murmured, taking in the keen blue eyes and the pleasant smile. He was leaning slightly toward his wife, also a pale blonde, although her hair had probably been tweaked a bit. In her mid-sixties as well, she looked as fit and trim as her husband.

"Beth," Angela recited.

The mother-in-law received a single nail tap. "She's a love. And this is Tim, my husband—Dr. Timothy Shilliday. His older sister Margaret—Dr. Shilliday-Ross (*tap-tap-tap*). And this is the baby. Julia. She broke the parents' hearts when she didn't follow her brother and sister into the family business. Medicine, that is. She's a massage therapist of all things."

Angela indicated a toothsome blonde, seated on the floor with an arm flung back and resting on her father's knee.

Nell felt like she'd just been served a large plate of cottage cheese.

"A beautiful family," she remarked as she passed the heavy photograph back. "It must be an amazing experience to sit for a Dorfman portrait."

"I'm looking forward to that experience myself," Angela agreed. "We're just waiting for the girls to get a tad older."

She served up the second photograph to Nell who obediently studied the composed portrait of the Timothy Shillidays—Tim again, two small girls with extraordinarily blonde hair, and Angela in the center, smiling enormously.

"What adorable little girls," Nell commented. "Tow heads."

"Yes. Blonde is a dominant gene, apparently, among the

Shillidays. I'm thinking of getting a chocolate lab—something that looks more like me."

The two women laughed.

"Well," said Angela suddenly turning brusque, "we'd better get down to business here. I am interested to know just what you can contribute to my project as a ghostwriter."

"And I," said Nell, "am eager to learn about your project."

Chapter 2

"I am in the middle of writing a book," Angela Shilliday said importantly. "A biography of Dr. Andrew Povitch. Do you know the name?"

Nell, rifling her mental files, frowned.

"I'm not quite sure. Nobel Prize? That's the only thing that pops up in my mind."

"Yes, exactly," said Angela. "Dr. Povitch shared the Nobel Prize for economic studies four years ago. He had been at Harvard but he had just come to Taft University to teach and to continue his ground-breaking work in economics."

Nell nodded. Comment didn't seem called for.

"I am writing his *authorized* biography," Angela continued, with a note of authority. "Other books can be written about Dr. Povitch—and probably are being written even as I speak—but mine has Andrew's imprimatur. That gives it special status."

"*Let it be printed,*" Nell murmured. "How did you win this plum? It sounds like a number of writers would like to be in your position."

"Yes. Many would. However, I met Andrew—Dr. Povitch—when I was doing my graduate studies. I guess my work and my writing caught his eye, and we became quite well acquainted. When I approached him about writing the biography, he immediately said yes."

Angela leaned back in her desk chair looking, Nell thought, rather satisfied with herself.

Nell cleared her throat. "I am slightly unclear about something."

Angela Shilliday raised her eyebrows, inviting Nell's question.

"If Dr. Povitch has appointed *you* to write his authorized biography, what am *I* doing here?"

"Ah, I was getting to that." Angela leaned toward Nell. "As you can probably imagine, I lead an insanely busy life."

She gestured toward the family room beyond the open door.

"Two little girls—Belinda is in first grade and Bianca is still in preschool. And besides getting them back and forth to school, there are dancing lessons, gym classes, and now Belinda wants to take tai kwon do and join a Daisy troop. I have a teaching schedule—two classes a week at Taft with all the preparation and paperwork *that* requires, plus this fourteen-room house to manage. Of course, I have help, but still, and as a prominent doctor's wife, there's all *that* entails. And in my spare time," she laughed, "I'm supposed to be writing my doctoral thesis. Well, in short, it doesn't leave much time for writing and I am slipping behind on my deadlines."

Nell could sympathize.

"And are you an economist too?"

"Exactly. And it was in an economics class that I met Andrew. He was brilliant. *Is,* I mean, *is* brilliant."

Angela smiled. Brilliantly.

Nell shifted in her chair. She was slightly bothered.

"Will Dr. Povitch be aware of me? Of my work? Will he recognize that you're presenting the work of a ghostwriter?"

"It won't be obvious that a ghost is involved. I mean, this will be more a collaboration, won't it? I assume you will write what I tell you; you'll present me with the drafts which I will review and I will indicate edits and oversee changes as needed. You will simply be channeling *me*, essentially. And I will pay you to be exactly what you are—a ghostwriter. Emphasis on ghost. Isn't that how you work? Anonymously?"

"I accept no credit lines on the published pieces I write," Nell said, "although sometimes the "author" mentions me in the acknowledgements. I am paid—compensated generously—in return for delivering a written piece, be it a book, an article, or whatever. If you wish to keep me 'under the covers'—no pun intended, that is fine as long as your checks cash."

Angela nodded, mollified. "That's what I'd understood."

But Nell was still uncomfortable. Angela Shilliday's concept of how one worked with a ghostwriter was somewhat off the mark. Off Nell's mark anyway. Nell had a premonition that this client could be difficult, but she shook off the warning instinct. The challenge of writing the biography of a Nobel Prize-winner was appealing.

"Now," said Angela, "with all that settled, tell me about your ghostwriting."

"Well," Nell began, "we would schedule several meetings early in the project so I can get a solid grasp of the task. I will want to get a good look at the resources you intend to supply. You *will* supply me with resources, yes?"

Nell looked meaningfully at Angela, who quickly assured her that resources were abundant and available.

"Okay. I will review those, look over the draft you've completed to date and meet with you to give you my comments. I rely very heavily on interviews, so I hope you will provide a list of people who can supply personal anecdotes, color, that sort of thing. And I would expect—economic studies being the subject—that certain technical materials will be provided and that you will make yourself available to answer my questions and, where necessary, to educate me on the subject."

Throughout this speech, Angela Shilliday had been nodding her agreement.

"I'll be able to be more definite," summarized Nell, "when I've looked at your material."

"And your payment? What do you charge? How do you get paid?"

"Until I understand the scope of the work ahead, I can't give you a hard-and-fast number," Nell said, "but I require payments in thirds. One third to begin the work, the second payment two-thirds of the way through the project—that determination to be made by me when I believe we have reached that mark—and the balance will be due when the final draft of the manuscript is delivered."

"I think that's acceptable," said Angela Shilliday, assuming her businesswoman model. "When can we begin? I am, understandably, in a hurry to get this project to the finish line."

Chapter 3

"Robert, have you heard of Andrew Povitch?"

"The Nobel Prize-winning economist? Sure."

"I needn't have asked," Nell grumbled. "How 'bout you, Jerry?"

"Me? Hell no." replied Jerry Gasso. "The cover teasers on the mags at the supermarket check-out lines are all I read. Robert, on the other hand, reads the actual *news*. He's the brains of the duo. And he files every factoid in that photographic memory of his."

Robert Hutchins gave Jerry a look.

"And why do you ask?" Robert wanted to know.

Nell sighed.

"I have a new fish on the line. A very interesting fish, to be sure, but there always seem to be trade-offs. This client comes with some baggage."

"I'm intrigued," Robert said. "Tell us."

And so Nell did.

Robert was tapping his chin with his forefinger when she

finished the story, but in typical Robert-fashion, he was silent. Nell poked him verbally.

"Well? I'd like to hear your opinions, comments, and condemnations."

Robert gave his chin several more taps, including a final thump that told Nell, reading his body language, that he was ready to speak.

"First," said Robert Hutchins, "I would, as you did, question the young lady about her ethical take on hiring a ghostwriter. Not," he said quickly, "that there's anything unethical about ghostwriters, but in this case she's not being up-front with her client. She's keeping you—the ghostwriter—locked in the closet. That, in and of itself, is not a necessarily a matter of ethics perhaps; it just isn't open and above-board."

Nell started to speak, but Robert held up a staying hand.

"I'm not finished."

He resumed tapping however, and the other two waited in silence.

"The ethical issue," he continued, "is not your concern. You aren't breaching any moral standard by taking the job."

"But if I am knowingly participating in a scheme where ethics may be compromised—and I have knowledge of this—doesn't that implicate me?"

"Implicate?" Robert gave a wry smiled. "Isn't that a strong word to use?"

Well," Nell conceded, trying again, "doesn't that load some of the responsibility onto me?"

"Nell, are you arguing against yourself? Testifying against your own case?"

Nell was sullenly silent.

"I'm confused," she admitted finally. "You know, Robert, I've always tried to walk the high moral ground."

Robert actually grinned.

"Just a few months ago—and over my strident objections, by the way—you gave back two-thirds of the money you'd worked long and hard for when you found out the payment for the book you'd been writing may have come—and I stress the word may—from ill-gotten gains. When it was revealed that your client was skimming money from the charity he'd established, you felt you couldn't keep the money you'd accepted in good faith for writing his book."

Nell nodded miserably. This was true.

"Tell me this," Robert probed, "are you feeling a bit pinched financially? Is that why, when you catch a whiff of ethical squashiness, you are willing to stick around instead of climbing onto that white marble plinth of yours and taking that morally exalted outlook?"

"Oh Robert, I don't know. I really don't. I guess I need to think long and hard about this. I think I need to look at the material Angela Shilliday has in place, and I need to learn more about the situation before I rush to judgment or before I accept the job."

"I think you should," Robert agreed. "And I think you should take your time. And I also think you shouldn't be so hard on yourself."

"Does anyone want to know what I think?" Jerry asked.

They looked at him.

"I think we should get our coats. And then I think we should walk up Charles Street and have dinner at Toscano. And I think we should order a bottle of Chianti Reserva and some terrific Tuscan food. And I think we should speak no more this evening of Angela Shilliday or of Nobel Prize winners."

"Jerry," said Robert, getting to his feet, "that's the best suggestion I've heard in this whole discussion."

Chapter 4

Angela Shilliday seemed somewhat scattered, Nell thought. Or distracted. She wasn't sure which, but the woman who held open the front door seemed almost surprised to see her.

"Oh! Oh, here you are already!" She squinted at Nell. "Are you early?"

"No," Nell told her, stepping in. "Right on time. We did agree to meet at 10:30, didn't we?"

"Oh! Yes, yes. Of course. Well...come on up."

And Angela Shilliday turned and took the front stairs two at a time. Nell followed more sedately and on the second floor, they switched staircases and Nell continued up the back stairs in Angela's wake.

"If you'll give me just a second or two," Angela said by way of explanation, waving Nell into her study, "I'll just...I have to... well, I'll only be a sec."

And she was off. Nell heard running feet on the stair. She slid her jacket off her shoulders and after looking around for a moment, decided to hang it over the back of a chair. Then she sat in the chair and inventoried the room.

A pride of bookcase loomed along one wall. There were books, of course, but an equal number of objects that Nell thought of as bits-and-bobs—mementoes and souvenirs and simply pretty things that had taken their owner's eye for one reason or another. Among the framed photographs, one in particular drew Nell's attention. She stood and walked over to examine it. In the photo a solid-looking man was laughing into the camera lens. The arm he had around Angela Shilliday was pulling her strongly against his chest. Angela was looking blissful—like a cat in the sun. Nell wondered if this was Dr. Andrew Povitch, the Nobel Prize-winning economist. If she'd been asked to write a description of an economist, she would have made him slight of frame and wispy-haired. Bespectacled, of course, and shy-looking, like he'd rather be anywhere than at a party. Angela's photo companion seemed to be having an excellent time at this gathering, though, and he looked like he could wrestle a bear and win.

She returned to her chair. She gazed out the window. She examined a pot of pens and pencils. She looked at the Dorfman photo that had caught her eye on the first visit to this study. An amazing-looking family, she decided. They could have sold the photo rights to a stock house or to Proctor and Gamble for a toothpaste ad.

The seconds ticked by. Nell watched them tick on a convenient clock placed on Angela's desk, and she wondered why she was being kept waiting. When 10:35 had ticked its way to 10:55, Nell uncrossed left leg from her right and with some impatience tossed the right leg over the left. The house was silent. Nell rose and went to the open door and surveyed the deserted rec room. Ah, she heard a distant voice she took to be Angela's scolding someone in the house—perhaps a child—and then she hear more running on the stairs.

"Whew!" said Angela Shilliday. This was all the explanation or apology Nell was to receive. "Well. Let's not waste time. We'll get started, shall we?"

Nell couldn't think of any retort to this, so she sat meekly down in the chair that held her jacket. Angela arranged herself in her desk chair and looked across at Nell.

"Well? Where do we start?"

"I believe you agreed to supply me with the resources you've been using to draft the Povitch biography. I'd like to see what you have. You also indicated that you've made a start on the manuscript. I want to see your outline and I'd especially like to read the draft so I can see how you're handling the material and so I can understand the voice you're using."

"Voice?" Angela asked.

Nell was surprised a writer would ask this question, but she obligingly answered, "You know, your style. Are you writing in the first person or the third? Are you being formal or informal? That sort of thing."

"Oh, of course," Angela nodded. "We'll want your writing to be compatible with mine."

"Yes."

"Well, give me a few minutes to just round up all the material, then you can be off to study it."

"I thought it would all be collected," Nell said in mild surprise.

"It'll just take a minute. Or a few minutes,"

And Angela Shilliday began opening and closing desk drawers and scrabbling around on the bookshelves. Apparently she kept her material in various places and Nell watched her perform an arabesque to reach a high shelf that held a slender sheaf of paper. Nell was reminded of the schoolroom game "hunt the thimble." Meanwhile the pile of papers on the end of the desk was growing.

"Oops!" Angela cried as the top layer slid sideways and littered itself on the floor. Nell also dropped to her hands and knees and together they harvested the scattered papers. Angela tapped these in a makeshift pile and flung a few books and a binder on the stack and stood back.

"Do you have transcripts of interviews you've done?" Nell asked.

It was a test.

For a few seconds Angela looked blank. She scrambled to recover her *sang-froid.*

"Oh, stuff like that is all included in there," she said, indicating the material she'd collected.

She pushed her hair back from her face with both hands.

"That's most of it," she declared.

Nell eyed the inventory somewhat warily.

"I have my briefcase," she said, "but..."

"Of course!" cried Angela, anticipating Nell's quandary. "I'll just nip down and get a box."

And once again she was off. And once again Nell thought of the hurrying, disappearing White Rabbit.

Returning with a carton that advertised Mondavi merlot, Angela hastily packed the inventory into it and loaded the carton in Nell's arms.

"You really must take care with this," she instructed. "It's got absolutely all my work—*everything!*—in it."

She led the way out of the office, though the rec room and down both sets of stairs. Nell trotted along, burdened with the carton. It was surprisingly heavy.

"You okay now?" Angela Shilliday called from the door as Nell jimmied the Mondavi carton into her car. "You need help or anything?"

"No," Nell called back, breathing a little harder than usual. "No, I've got it. I'm okay."

Chapter 5

"My god!" exclaimed Bunty Whitney, pushing through the back door. "What's all this then? Looks like the recycling center had a revolution."

"My potential client, Angela Shilliday, landed me with her resources," explained Nell. "The stuff meant to craft the biography of Dr. Andrew Povitch."

Bunty surveyed the stacks of paper arranged on the island. Then her eyes swiveled to the counters beside the sink on which were arranged rows of carrots, leeks, potatoes, a huge swash of parsley and one lumpy turnip.

"And that?"

"The makings for Golden Vegetable Soup," Nell explained tiredly. "I felt so swamped and overwhelmed by all of Angela's clobber that all I could think to do was make soup."

Bunty, long familiar with her neighbor's soup therapy, nodded.

"How 'bout if I peel those spuds and carrots and you can tell me all about this new client?"

So while Bunty peeled and chopped—and while Nell pretended not to notice that Bunty was clopping out great, mismatched hunks of vegetable—Nell described the big gray stucco house in Winchester with its ballroom-sized rooms and jaw-dropping window treatments. Then she went on to describe Angela Shilliday. When she got to the part about being the secret ghostwriter, Bunty put down the paring knife and turned from the sink to stare.

"Let me get this straight. This Dr. Povitch hired *her* to write his biography, right?"

"Right."

"Because he—what?—admired her writing style? Her knowledge of economics? Her legs?"

"Probably all three."

"Okay. But he doesn't know she's not going to be doing the writing? That she's hiring someone else to write?"

"Correct."

Bunty scowled.

"I don't get it."

"I'm not sure I get it either," Nell admitted with a sigh. "In fact, I'm not even sure I'm going to accept the job. I'm going to read the material Angela has supplied, then make up my mind."

Bunty turned back to the sink.

"Okay," she said, "That sounds reasonable. She sounds kind of crazy though, this Angela Shilliday."

Nell's eyebrows went up.

"Bunty! Is that anyway for a psychotherapist to talk?"

"Potter," Bunty corrected. "Potter. I'm a recovering psychotherapist. That was another life."

For a time the kitchen was silent except for the sound of Bunty's chopping.

"Do you actually like these things?" she asked suddenly,

turning from the sink again.

Nell looked up from her sorting. Bunty was holding up a wedge of yellow vegetable.

"Rutebaga?"

"Is that what you call it? I thought it was turnip."

"Same thing essentially."

"I think they're vile," Bunty pronounced.

"They're okay," Nell replied. "I kind of like them."

"Takes all kinds," Bunty responded gloomily and returned to her task.

GOLDEN VEGETABLE SOUP

12 oz. of carrots, peeled and chopped
1 rutabaga, chopped
2 small leeks, washed and sliced
1 large russet potato, diced
3-4 cups of vegetable stock
1 cup of milk
1/4 cup of heavy cream
1 tablespoon of chopped parsley

Nell was planning to combine all the vegetables with the stock in a large saucepan. When this boiled, she'd turn down the heat, cover the pot and simmer the soup for 30 minutes. Next, she'd use an immersion blender to puree the mixture. Finally, she'd stir in the milk and reheat the soup, seasoning it with salt and pepper.

When the soup was ready to serve, Nell would whip the cream into soft peaks and fold 1 tablespoon of chopped parsley into the cream to make an herb Chantilly for a garnish.

Chapter 6

Nell was sorting Angela's material into suites. "Like playing a giant game of bridge," she thought. There was a biographical pile where everything about Dr. Andrew Povitch's personal life was stacked. There was an area for research material on economics, including Povitch's special area of ecological economics, and another section for reference material on the Nobel Prize itself. Finally there was Angela's area with her first draft of the biography and her outlines and notes. The island in the kitchen was soon covered in paper, and Nell started carrying material into the dining room and making stacks on the table there.

Rain began to ping on the windows and Nell was glad. If she had to hunker down with all this clobber, she'd just as soon enjoy being sealed inside, and the typical three-day blow of a nor'easter suited her just fine.

"Who is Andrew Povitch," Nell murmured, "that all our maids adore him?"

Deciding to start with Angela's unfinished draft of the

biography, she tucked herself into the corner of the sofa in the snug and under the gooseneck lamp, began to read.

Four typed pages into the draft Nell lifted her head. She removed her reading glasses and sighed deeply. Angela Shilliday's writing style was pretentious and inflated. Where one or two words could handle a task, Angela used eight or nine. Where a single syllable word would have been the strong, Angela diluted the prose with a multisyllabic choice.

"She must have consulted a thesaurus to scour out every possible overblown word," Nell muttered in disgust.

Angela Shilliday was much given to hyperbole and was extremely fond of exclamation points. Sighing again, Nell put the reading glasses back on and resumed reading.

But a funny thing began to happen. With each new page, the writing style changed; it withered, offered less detail, and by page 20—the last typed page—had been reduced to sentence fragments and mere notes. Several handwritten pages—hastily scribbled—were appended to the draft, and much sooner than expected, Nell found herself sitting on the sofa in the snug, staring in amazement at the sheaf of papers in her lap.

She was starting to understand why Angela Shilliday had called in a ghostwriter.

"She is incapable of this writing job," Nell told herself. "It is simply beyond her ability. She has bitten off much more than she can chew."

Angela's outline was predictable. It listed a section of Povitch's background—childhood, education, that sort of thing. Angela planned to narrate his economic studies and his introduction to and interest in the ecological branch of economics. And, of course, it would culminate in the drama of receiving the Nobel Prize for Economics.

Nell shuffled through the resource material. There seemed

to be plenty of information—stuff that Nell thought of as grist for the mill. But searching for the interviews that Angela had already conducted, brought Nell up short. There didn't seem to be any at all. Interviews, Nell felt, were the lifeblood of a biography and most biographers interviewed extensively.

Well, disappointing perhaps, but Nell would arrange her own interviews. It was good that Andrew Povitch was local and that there would be plenty of people at Taft who could add enlightenment. Beefed up with the personal interviews and with the material still to be mined, she was confident she could make something of this biography project.

The only log in the road, then, was the author herself— Angela Shilliday.

Could she work with Angela? Would their personalities mesh or clash? As associates in this project—as co-conspirators sort of—they would become close. But did Nell want to become close with Angela Shillliday?

She wasn't sure of the answers to any of these questions— or perhaps reservations was the better word than questions— but she did recognize that the chance to write the biography of Dr. Andrew Povitch was shining in in her vision as the Holy Grail must have shone in the dazzled imaginations of Arthur's knights. And Nell had a strong suspicion about what she'd do. About the choice she'd make. She could postpone or delay, but in the end, she wouldn't be able to resist the challenge. She wouldn't be able to keep herself away. She wandered to the window and looked at the rain turning the street to a shining pond under the street lamp. And she felt doomed.

Chapter 7

"I'm doing it Robert," she told her confessor.

"Ah," her old friend replied. "I'd suspected the bait of this Povitch thing would prove to tasty too resist. Tell me about it."

Nell remembered a caution she'd heard a kindergarten teacher give years before. "When you are viewing the artwork of a small child." the woman had said, "whether it is a big painting created in gobs of schoolroom tempera or simply a drawing done with one orange crayon, you never, ever say, 'What is it?' You mustn't insult the young artist by admitting you don't recognize the subject. Rather, say: 'Tell me about it.'"

Nell smiled now at the way Robert had framed his question, and she considered once again his patience with her and for her. And she silently blessed him.

"Her own writing is C to C-minus level," Nell said bluntly. "It's good enough to get by and be forgiven but it is not professional standard. Left to her own devices, I seriously doubt she could ever write an entire book. So all that talk about being too busy and too important to do the grunt work of book-writing is nonsense. I think she believes the nonsense though. I think she contacted me, not because she wanted to but because she didn't want to lose face at this point and admit to Povitch that she wasn't up to the task."

"Does she have decent material to work with?" Robert wanted to know.

"Well, she has certainly collected a lot of stuff," Nell said. "Some of it is bound to be worthwhile. Of course, I'll set up some interviews—with Povitch of course and with his associates, people who knew him 'when', that sort of thing. The inferior writing style can be corrected and overcome. No, it's not Angela's writing I'm concerned about."

"Ah," said Robert, sounding wise. "Now we come too the nut. What *are* you concerned about, Nell?"

Nell didn't know whether to be annoyed that Robert could read her so well, or relived and grateful that he could. She decided to be grateful.

"It's Angela herself. She seems to wear different faces at different times. Or maybe I mean different personalities." Nell considered. "I don't know," she continued, "maybe it's just me."

Robert listened without comment. Long experience had taught him that Nell would reach her own conclusions in her own time.

And she did.

"Oh well," she announced briskly. "Like the Six Hundred, I'm riding into the Valley of Death. Wish me Godspeed, Robert."

Robert did.

Chapter 8

In a carefully composed email, Nell sent word to Angela Shilliday that she would accept the job of ghostwriting the biography of Dr. Andrew Povitch, conditional upon Angela's acceptance of Nell's terms. Nell presented her estimate to do the job with one-third of the money to be paid upon starting the project, the second third to be due at mid-point (that point to be determined by Nell Bane) and the final payment due when the finished manuscript was delivered to the client.

"The die is cast," murmured Nell, trying to remember her first year Latin. And failing to remember, continued, "Thus we cross the Rubicon."

And she hit "Send."

Nell checked her email rather more frequently than usual in the next several days, but there was no response from Angela Shilliday.

"Nothing is lost," Nell told Bunty. "I'm not out anything except a bit of my time. And the cost of the gas to drive that wine box full of clobber back to Winchester."

"Damn," Bunty replied. "I was looking forward to the drama of this project."

"To learning all about Andrew Povitch?"

"That, yes. But I wanted to know more about Angela Shilliday. She intrigues me, that one. There's a story there and it may be a better story than Andrew Povitch's biography."

"You'll be the first to know when I hear from Angela Shilliday."

"*If* you hear from Angela Shilliday," Bunty said maliciously. And she had the nerve to grin at Nell.

But then Nell did hear. And Angela Shilliday was accepting Nell's terms—and her price. She stated that they needed to meet again very soon because time on this project was "of the essence," and she gave Nell two dates in her very busy schedule when this meeting could happen. Nell was to pick one and confirm by email immediately.

"Huh," said Nell.

Now, on the approved date, Nell guided the Saab into Winchester and into the complicated triangular arrangement of streets where Washington connects with Skillings and Mt. Vernon. Waiting for the lights to change, Nell contemplated some of the town's handsomely endowed churches and its imposing town hall and public library, all bespeaking affluence. She continued across Mystic Valley Parkway and down Main where residences replaced public buildings, and pulled up shortly at the Shilliday address.

But it wasn't Angela Shilliday who answered Nell's ring. The door was opened by a woman whom Nell took to be a housekeeper.

"Hello, I'm Nell Bane." She extended her hand. "I have an appointment with Angela Shilliday."

"Glorimar," the woman told her. She pronounced the name in three distinct syllables, offered an incandescent smile and shook Nell's hand. Nell was helpless. She smiled too

"Missus Shilliday said to go on upstairs. She said you knew the way."

Nell did know the way, and as she climbed the front stairs, then trooped down the long upstairs hall past open bedroom doors, she considered that she was privy to the underbelly of the Shillliday house—to the wrenched-looking toothpaste tube on the sink and the puddle of pajama pants on the bedroom floor where their owner had stepped out of them that morning. The intimate view conferred privilege, and she resisted the urge to peek into the snoratorium. Looking straight ahead so as to avoid temptation to voyeurism, Nell mounted the backstairs and headed for the open door of Angela's study.

"Oh hello there," Angela Shilliday said musically.

She was wearing glasses. They were becoming, Nell thought; they gave her a more approachable air.

"I was just doing lesson plans," Angela explained. She sighed, removed the glasses and ran both hands through her hair, pushing it back. "I've got exactly one hour before I have to dash out, so I'd like to accomplish as much as possible."

This put Nell slightly on the defensive. Had she taken too much time walking through the house, thus compromising their schedule?

"We'd better begin then," she said, seating herself across from Angela's desk. "The first thing I'd like to do is gather some background."

Angela nodded.

"I'd like to start with a bit about your background so I can learn how you came to know Dr. Povitch."

Angela seemed mildly surprised by this request but she nodded again.

"Okay. I met Andrew—Dr. Povitch—shortly after coming to Taft as an undergraduate."

"What were you studying?" Nell interrupted.

"At the time, I was a history major. I didn't have any interest in economics for quite a while. In fact, it was Dr. Povitch's influence that made me switch majors in my senior year. I signed up for one of his lectures and I was hooked on the subject. Forever and always!"

"Where were you from?"

Again, Angela looked surprised.

"Michigan. Why? Is that relevant?"

"Probably not," Nell said equitably. "Just a point of reference for me. So you'd come east to school."

"Yes," Angela said shortly.

"Go on," encouraged Nell.

Angela was still frowning at her. "Where was I?"

"At Dr. Povitch's lecture. You were becoming infatuated with economics."

"Infatuated isn't the word I'd use," Angela said.

Nell waited to hear the word she *would* use. And indeed, Angela seemed to be searching for it too. Then she dismissed the subject with a wave.

"More to the point, I found the subject engrossing. It was almost an epiphany. I changed my major and decided I'd go on to grad school."

"And what did you plan to do after that? As an economist, I mean," Nell asked.

"I thought I'd probably do something in Washington," Angela said rather vaguely. "For a while anyway, then I knew I'd probably end up teaching."

She spread her hands over the papers on her desk.

"And, *voila*, it came to pass. I'm in the classroom two days a week."

"But you're also a wife," Nell pointed out. "And the mother of two little girls. You're a lot more than a teacher."

Angela acknowledged this with a series of modest nods.

"And now an author," Nell prompted gently. "Tell me how that part of the story came about."

Angela Shilliday was visibly pleased to field this question.

"Well, Andrew knew me from his classes, of course. And I flatter myself to think that the papers I wrote impressed him. He said as much when we'd meet in his office for conferences. I earned a position as a graduate assistant, which put me on a similar footing with Andrew. Well, only in a manner of speaking, of course. He was a tenured professor and I was hanging on the lowest rung of the economics department, but still..."

Angela trailed off. Nell waited. She was good at waiting.

"After I earned my Masters," Angela continued, picking up the thread, "I did go to Washington where I worked for a while in the commerce department. It wasn't very challenging work, if you want to know. Quite dull, really, and I was eager to get back to Boston. For one thing, there was a handsome young cardiologist I was seeing."

She smiled.

"Dr. Timothy Shilliday," Nell supplied.

"That's right. But I was also drawn back to Taft and began my doctoral work."

Nell was impressed.

"Ah, two doctors in the family then."

"Not quite. Babies interrupted the work on my dissertation. I went back at it briefly after Belinda but then Bianca came along and the balance of diapers-to-doctorate tipped again. I am starting back on the thesis though," she added hastily.

Angela's cell phone chimed and she snatched it up and squinted at the text message, then quickly tapped a response.

"That's going to be it for today," she announced, standing up. "I've got to dash. You can see yourself out, can't you? Just tell Glorimar you're going."

And Angela Shilliday vanished.

Nell considered grumpily that she had accommodated her client by agreeing to this time, that she had driven all the way down from Newburyport—a drive of forty-five minutes when the traffic was cooperative—and, facing the long drive in reverse, She would be carrying and was going to carry away only a meager amount of information.

Chapter 9

Home once again, and with the pitifully small deposit of information about the project, Nell reasoned that she'd have to start scratching up research on her own.

"The charge for the day," she told herself, "is to get to know Dr. Andrew Povitch."

She knew two things about him: that he had been awarded the Nobel Prize for his work in ecological economics and that he admired the writing of Angela Shilliday. The first fact was documented. The second was hearsay.

Andrew Povitch, she learned, was born in Cleveland of Slovenian parents who immigrated to the United States as displaced persons just after the second world war. Cleveland, she found out, had the greatest population of Slovenians outside of Slovenia itself.

Nell had to brush up on the geography of Slovenia. She consulted a map and learned it was in Central Europe with Austria to its north, Italy to the west and Croatia to the south.

Since Frank and Anna Povitch had a few relatives and

plenty of countrymen in the Collinwood area just east of Cleveland, they were soon a solid part of the community's fabric and ready to establish their family. So along came young Andrew Povitch, and for him, home was the top half of a two-family house on East 143rd Street, near Five Points. His dad worked at the Fisher Body plant, his mother was active in the sodality at St. Mary's church, and the whole family enjoyed socializing at the local Slovenian National Home—one of nine such "homes" established in the late 1800s and early 1900s, to offer Slovenian culture and social opportunities. Andrew must have played with the neighborhood kids and attended countless wedding receptions at the Home. Through the eighth grade, he attended St. Mary's school, but high school was Collinwood High, and there Andrew Povitch shone. He was recognized as a popular, outgoing and outstanding student, and was elected to National Honor Society, voted class president and named valedictorian.

Povitch earned a scholarship to The Ohio State University and after his undergraduate years in Columbus, never really returned to Cleveland. A week after graduation, he headed east to continue his studies at various prestigious universities.

His father died in 1971 while Povitch was attending a conference in Switzerland. His mother died the following year, and with her death the few remaining tethers to his hometown were broken.

Nell wanted—needed—more. She went prowling online for more—some interview, some humanizing stories, *something* that would make Dr. Andrew Povitch more than a list of statistics. The best she could find was an interview that appeared in *The Cleveland Plain Dealer* shortly after the Nobel Prize was announced.

Dr. Andrew Povitch hasn't been back to Cleveland in years, but he still retains a deep fondness for his native city, along with great pride in his Slovenian heritage.

"Walking back and forth to school—first to St. Mary's then later to Collinwood High—I'd be thinking of food. A lot of people grew their own grapes in backyards and in the fall, when school started up again, the streets smelled like a vineyard. As a kid, I was always hungry, and the first thing I'd shout when I got in the door was, "Ma, I'm home. What's for supper? My mother's goveja juha was the best!" (Note to non-Slovenian readers: Slovenian beef broth).

"Yes, food was a big thing in the neighborhood. Azman Meats over on East 185th was where we got smoked meats and klobase (sausage). There were any number of bakeries, but for potica, the best—next to my mother's—was Wojtila's ."

"I also have great memories of Euclid Beach, the big old amusement park down on Lake Shore Boulevard near East 156th. It's gone now, but I bet I rode for miles on the Racing Coaster and the Flying Turns. I remember this huge dummy—actually there were two outside the Fun House—that just stood there and laughed and laughed. Wherever you went at Euclid Beach, that's what you heard—laughing."

Andrew Povitch may have the Nobel Prize for Economics, but he also has great memories of Cleveland.

Well, it was something anyway, this interview. More than the sterile encyclopedic facts Angela had collected. But Slovenian beef broth had made Nell hungry. And curious. She went on a recipe search for goveja juha.

This dish, according to the recipe, was the lifeblood of the Slovenian dinner, especially the Sunday dinner where it stimulated the appetite. Complex and interesting, it is "magnificently nutritious" and it "lingers and cavorts on the tongue," Nell read.

"My, my," she murmured. "Cavorts, does it?"

She knew she couldn't leave this recipe alone.

GOVEJA JUHA
SLOVENIAN BEEF SOUP

1 and 1/2 pounds of good beef
1/2 pound beef bones with good marrow
8-10 cups water
1 Tablespoon salt
2 Tablespoons butter
1/4-1/2 pounds beef liver, sliced into cubes (optional)
2 carrots, unpeeled and chopped
2 stalks celery, chopped
1 onion, chopped
a cabbage stem or a turnip or cauliflower core
1 bay leaf
1 heaping teaspoon black peppercorns
1/4 teaspoon saffron, heated to brittleness, then dissolved
in hot water (optional)
1 cup cold water

Nell read that she could add 2 cups of cooked rice or 2 cups of soup noodles, or perhaps some sautéed mushrooms. If she chose not to add any of these, she had the option of breaking a raw egg into each bowl before ladling in the soup.

She was to rinse the beef and bones and place them in a large pot with 8-10 cups of cold water. This she was to a simmer very slowly. And she was NOT to skim the brown foam, for the foam will eventually sink and strengthen the broth. In the meantime, she should melt the butter in a pan and stir in the liver and vegetables, frying them to a golden color. The liver and vegetables, along with the salt, were then to be added to the broth. And the frying pan was to be washed with broth and drained into the soup which should cook gently for at least 2 hours.

While the broth was simmering, the noodles, rice or mushrooms were to be cooked in a separate pot and would sit until the soup was ready to serve.

When the meat was cooked, Nell was to pour a teacup of cold water into the broth to clear it, then leave it to cool. Next she was to pass the soup through a fine strainer, then refrigerate it to make the fat easy to remove.

When the soup was ready to serve, it should be heated to a full boil, and the rice, noodles or mushrooms would be added and heated. The soup was to be served in small bowls or, Nell learned it was permissible to break a raw egg into each bowl before ladling in the soup.

Nell carefully added the recipe to her soup book, where she could find it when she was ready to attempt the complex recipe.

Chapter 10

The shopkeepers of Newburyport were hurrying the season. Apparently they couldn't wait to heave out the pumpkins and bittersweet vines of autumn. The window boxes in front of the shops along State Street already had thrusts of mixed evergreens and alderberries. You couldn't blame them though, the shopkeepers. This was the fat season—the time when Christmas made their cash registers ring.

The weather was unseasonably warm for the fat season, and Nell, striding along, needed nothing more than her heavy sweater to stay snug. She was meeting Robert for lunch at Agave, so midway up State Street, she turned and climbed the inside stairs to the Mexican restaurant. It was late, and the lunch crowd had thinned considerably, which was fine with Nell. Food was secondary today. Mostly she wanted the chance for a deep-dish conversation with her old friend Robert Hutchins.

"So what do you know about Andrew Povitch?" Robert asked as he flapped open his napkin and laid it precisely on his lap.

"I know how to make goveja juha," Nell answered somewhat bitterly. "And I know that *potica*—pronounced po-*TEET*-sa—is a nut-filled pastry."

"That sounds only marginally useful," Robert observed. "Surely there's more than that."

"Oh, to be sure! It's just that I haven't found it yet. I hadn't expected to do this much digging, Robert. I should have named a higher price for this job."

"And where are you excavating at present?"

"I'm deep in the dingles of economics," Nell sighed. "English majors stay away from economics as a rule. I may be over my head in this."

"You'll prevail," Robert told her tranquilly. "You always do."

He studied the menu for several minutes, and then closed it looking satisfied.

"You've decided?"

"Ceviche apulqueno," he announced.

Nell shuddered. "Raw fish!"

"Halibut. And it's not raw. The lemon juice cooks it. And you?"

"Sopa de tortilla," she said, "and I could do with a Margarita."

"Tortilla soup," Robert said reflectively. "Predictable. Now. Give me an economics lesson."

"Economics 101," recited Nell as the Margaritas arrived. "Here goes. As near as I can tell, Povitch was a mainstream economist until the early 1970s when the whispers of climate change started up in earnest. Then people started worrying about acid rain and pollution, and various other ecological issues began blowing in the wind."

Robert looked pained. "Ouch. Terrible pun."

"Sorry," Nell grinned. "Anyhow, Povitch apparently

recognized that these two disciplines—ecology and economics—could be synergized and could thereby have a significant national and international effect. He began to travel to Europe to meet with like-minded scientists and economists, and subsequently he began writing and lecturing on the subject. Extensively. Writing and lecturing, that is, and he became one of the leading voices on the subject."

Nell paused to sip the Margarita and felt restored to a small degree. She set the glass down and continued.

"Povitch is, by all accounts, a charismatic man, both on and off the podium. Not only is his thought and his research sound, but it is fresh as well. And apparently he has the ability to deliver his ideas persuasively and compellingly. All in all, he is a very attractive package. He seems able to handle the give-and-take of small groups and, with equal ease, can hold the interest of auditoriums full of listeners, even when he's presenting the sort of scholarly papers, which all too often put people to sleep. In short, he became very well respected among his peers and was—and is—a highly popular professor when he lectures or offers a course."

"So tell me a little more about ecological economics," Robert said. "It sounds interesting but I'm fuzzy on exactly what it is."

"So am I," admitted Nell, "but this is what I think I've understood. Ecological economics is distinguished from plain, old mainstream economics because it emphasizes strong sustainability. Furthermore, it rejects the notion that natural capital can be substituted by man-made capital."

"My, my," murmured Robert. "Who knew?"

"Well, it focuses on nature," Nell continued, "and on justice and time as well. It looks at interactions between human beings and the natural world and then asks questions like: How does human behavior connect to changes in hydrological nutrients or carbon cycles? And what are the feedbacks between social and natural systems? Oh, and get this. Ecological economic is differentiated from *environmental* economics because it treats the economy as a subsystem of the ecosystem. You see?"

"Well, I'm not sure I do see," Robert admitted frankly. "And I'm impressed by what you've managed to assimilate in a short time."

"I'm just parroting what I've read," Nell sighed. "Like cramming for a test the night before the exam. I'll write what I have to and forget it all. Oh, look, lunch is here! Let's change the subject. Share some gossip with me, Robert. Jerry must have told you some juicy tidbits."

But over coffee, Robert opened the subject again.

"The Nobel Prize, there must be hundreds of whip-smart economists—thousands. Out of all of those, why did the Nobel committee settle on Andrew Povitch?"

Nell held her coffee mug delicately in both hands and rested her elbows on the table. The coffee smelled heavenly but it was too hot to drink.

"Tell me what you already know about the prize," Nell said.

"Well," Robert considered. "I know there is a committee in Sweden made up of people of some standing in various prestigious institutions. And I know they meet annually to nominate the winners and that there are six categories. Let me see if I can name them."

Robert's eyes travelled to Agave's ceiling as if the list could be read there.

"There's medicine," he read from his memory, "and chemistry. Literature. Peace, of course. Economics— obviously—and, let's see, what am I missing?"

"Physics," Nell supplied. "And the peace prize, by the way, isn't part of the regular selection process. A separate committee meets to name the peace prize winner. Interesting factoid: the regular committee meets in Sweden, but for some reason Alfred Nobel specified that the peace prize be handled by a Norwegian committee. Another thing to know is that there is a committee for each disciple—which makes sense."

Robert nodded.

"But back to the original question," he said, "why Andrew Povitch?"

"There's some controversy and ongoing discussion about the selection processes apparently," Nell explained. "That's what I'm gathering from my reading anyway. Some argue that the process is too subjective; that it's based on the opinions and favorites of a few people on the committees. Another controversy is the complaint that the process favors individual careers over individual accomplishment. I certainly can't comment on that."

She auditioned the temperature of her coffee. Perfect.

"But now we're closing in on your question. It seems that the people who've won the prize tend to be published very heavily in the journals read by their peers. Furthermore, they tend to be well-known in their fields. The number of published papers and general work that stimulates further research in the named field are all considered vaulting poles that bring an individual closer to the eyes of a committee. Andrew Povitch has achieved a very high profile in his field. Amen."

Robert nodded once again, this time with an ah-ha sort of nod.

Seeing that he understood, Nell nodded also.

"Andrew Povitch," she said, "is by all accounts a personable, charismatic man. He is apparently an excellent speaker and lecturer and a jolly chum in the after-hours shoulder rubbing that goes on at every national and international conference and seminar. And he has published exhaustively. There isn't a journal in the field of ecological economics that hasn't printed his byline, and the promise of an Andrew Povitch article in a journal guarantees higher-than-normal readership. All of that contributes to a sizable share of mind among committee members. It would be virtually impossible for Andrew Povitch's name and reputation *not* to come up for discussion and consideration."

"What typically happens to a Nobel winner after the prize is awarded?" Robert wanted to know.

"What do you think? Laurels piled on laurels. There's a money prize, of course, but that is almost incidental. It's the prestige and publicity that catapults a winner on to greater glory. Fame, Robert, is a powerful aphrodisiac."

"He must be a fascinating man to know," Robert observed.

Nell suddenly looked grim.

"I wouldn't know," she said. "I have yet to meet him."

Chapter 11

"I feel like I'm working with a paper bag over my head," Nell complained to Angela Shilliday. "Or maybe Andrew Povitch has the paper bag over his head. But in either case, I'm writing in the dark. Is it possible for me to meet Dr. Povitch? Interview him?"

"Absolutely not," was the instant answer. "Out of the question."

Nell stared. Interviews were the life force of her writing. It gave a story immediacy and interest, pace and vitality. She was stunned.

She tried to explain this to her client.

"The thing is," Angela said, squirming slightly in her chair, "Andrew thinks—he must *believe*—that I am writing this book. He must depend on *me* to do it. I must remind you that I hired you to *ghost* write. You must be absolutely transparent, and if you interview Andrew, you'll blow the cover."

Nell was still silent, but her face must have communicated incredulity, because Angela Shilliday gave another squirm in her chair and changed the subject.

"Well," she slid her reading glasses onto her face. "Let's look at what you've been working on."

And Nell, swallowing her anger, opened her briefcase and produced the draft she'd done to date. And for a reasonably companionable half hour, she and Angela reviewed the copy and agreed to certain changes."

"I'm pretty pleased," Angela announced when the last page had been turned over. "Pleasantly surprised, actually, although you will have to amend the style in a number of places to be more consistent with the way I write."

She punctuated this remark with a sticky smile. Then, removing the glasses once more, she sat back.

"Okay," she said, "here's a compromise. Tim and I give this tremendous Christmas party every year. Everyone we know comes—Tim's associates, family, all my friends, people from the country club, well, *everyone*. Andrew will be there. Why don't you come to the party? You can observe Andrew for yourself. Meet him, maybe. Watch him. Have a quick chat with him—*but don't say who you are,*" she added hastily.

She had the grace to look embarrassed and added weakly, "but, you know, you can at least see him."

Nell allowed her silence to continue. It lay like an entity between the two women and the room was very still. Then she nodded crisply. The invitation was better than nothing. And she felt insulted. But she'd take it.

"Give me the date and time," Nell said.

Chapter 12

From the basement to the third floor, every Watt in the Shilliday house was at maximum. The front door bristled with an enormous wreath that must have cost a packet-and-a-half at Mahoney's, thought Nell as she brushed past it. Oh, but it smelled delicious! And she paused for a second to inhale the scent.

She stood, then, for several moments in the hall getting her bearings. The familiar house seemed unfamiliar on this night. There were holiday greens everywhere—twined up the stairs, bursting from urns and vases on every tabletop, and no fewer than three dramatic Christmas trees were placed strategically in the hall, the living room, and even in Tim Shilliday's study. Fairy lights, silver balls and yards of white satin ribbon were in evidence everywhere, and Nell couldn't imagine how Angela, who was always so busy-busy-busy, had managed this transformation.

Nell went in search of a glass of white wine—her standard party prop. A glass in your hand allowed you to blend into the conviviality while buying immunity from the good-hearted souls who were always offering to fetch you a drink. Nell only sipped white wine at these affairs in order to minimize the disastrous effects of red wine splashed or spilled by jostling party-hearty types.

"You must try a cup of Beth's Glogg," someone—a woman with earrings like huge silver snowflakes—commanded.

"You need to *experience* Glogg!" the woman enthused, slopping out a cupful for Nell. "And Beth's is amazing. She makes it with *figs!*"

Nell, who had endured the Glogg experience on several occasions and who didn't enjoy the mixture of red wine and brandy, thought ruefully of the glass of white wine she would now have to forego. But she smiled insincerely and accepted a cup of the warm, sweet punch that featured, as she'd feared it would, a nest of raisins and almonds in the bottom of the cup. The cup felt sticky.

But thus armed, she moved into the fray of the party, bent on observation and information—an undercover agent at the celebration.

It was easy to identify a Shilliday, Nell decided. Three generations were represented and their gene pool was strong. Tall, lean, blonde, excellent skin and teeth, the latter displayed in gleaming smiles that would have sent the pulse of a dental hygienist beating in joy.

Beth Shilliday, designer of the amazing Glogg, was wearing a white silk blouse and was busy refreshing trays of food, introducing people and administering motherly pats to all who came near. Thomas Shilliday, father-in-law of Angela and noted cardiologist, was chatting amiably with a group that looked to be entirely comprised of physicians, all of whom, apparently, participated in the same running group. Five mornings out of seven, 6:30 AM sharp. They all looked astoundingly fit.

Tim Shilliday, walking proof that the apple doesn't fall far from the tree, was a clone of his dad except three decades younger. He was wearing his hostly role with ease, rounding up guests and introducing them to other guests.

"I don't think we've met yet," he said, coming up to Nell. "Tim Shilliday."

He put out his hand.

Nell smiled. "I know you by reputation, of course," she said. "I'm Nell Bane. I'm working with your wife on her ... um ... project."

Dr. Shilliday laughed. "Yes, I know all about the book. But Angela will be pleased when I tell her how discreet you are. How's the work going?"

Nell gave a fleeting thought to telling him, then decided the gentle, social lie was a better choice for this evening. She smiled. "Well, I hope. As long as the client is pleased, the project is on track."

Tim Shilliday put a warm hand on her upper arm, perfectly cupping the deltoid, and gave a slight squeeze. Nell recognized this as the gesture of a physician ducking out of the examining room before overstaying the time allotment. Give the patient a physical sign, just intimate enough to reassure but not overly familiar, then get the hell out.

"Excellent," said Dr. Tim Shilliday. "Excellent. Pleased to hear it. Well, you enjoy the party. Get something good to eat. Have someone get you some of my mother's exceptional Glogg."

The ebb and flow of party guests never brought Nell into the orbit of Dr. Margaret Shilliday-Ross, Tim's older sister and respected vascular surgeon, but Nell did have a pleasant exchange with her husband, Dr. Michael Ross, who, as he modestly confessed, was "merely an ear, nose and throat man.

I don't move in the exalted circles of the heart, my dear."

Nell liked him. He had a twinkle, an endearing manner and a wonderful smile that featured an overlapping front tooth. Despite this imperfection, he'd been embraced into the Shilliday clan.

Julia Shilliday arrived late. The front door opened, admitting a blast of December air and a current of something indefinable. An electric charge instantly infused the guests and caused the party to undergo some sort of chemical change. Energy shifted into a higher gear. Nell heard a rippling soprano and a carol of laughter from the foyer, and then—there— stepping into the living room, was the baby of the family. At last.

She caught sight of her father across the room and with a little squeal of delight was in his arms. Julia Shilliday was easily six feet tall in tennis shoes, but this night she was wearing four-inch heels—about the same length as the hem of her little black dress, Nell calculated. It was a simple, elegant sheath that fell from the shoulders. Her only accessory was her straight blonde hair which hung to her shoulder blades and which she had learned to use to splendid advantage. She was a pleasure to watch, and Nell caught herself smiling.

Crying, "I must have some of Mummy's Glogg!" Julia Shilliday swept from the room, taking with her some of the energy or air. It appeared that the lamps had dimmed by several lumens.

But Nell was on a mission—a secret mission to identify Dr. Andrew Povitch and to study him from afar. Or from near, if she could manage it circumspectly.

"Do you happen to know if Dr. Andrew Povitch is here?" she asked the woman standing next to her against the dining room wall.

"It happens, I do," the woman replied, turning to look up

at Nell, her merry brown eyes snapping with amusement.

Nell was taken a bit aback. She was a petite woman herself, and it was unusual to meet someone shorter, but this woman barely reached five feet. Besides the merry eyes, she had crisp salt-and-pepper hair—short as a bathing cap—and a vitality that was equally crisp.

Nell, still slightly off balance, stared.

"Well, would you ... do you mind...?"

The woman's smile had an elfin quality.

"Not at all. *That's* Dr. Povitch, just there. The fellow helping himself to the ham."

Nell followed the direction of this woman's glance. So the man heartily forking slices of ham onto his place was Andrew Povitch. He was able, Nell noted, to go right at that ham and still keep up an animated conversation with the woman at his elbow who was dabbling in a bowl of pasta salad. As a unit, Povitch and his companion shifted right which brought the Nobel Prize winning economist to the pasta bowl and the unidentified woman to a dish of condiments.

Nell suddenly became aware that her new companion was watching her with amusement.

"I'm sorry," Nell stammered. "It's just that I know Dr. Povitch by reputation and I ..."

"Would you like an introduction?"

Nell was dumbstruck.

The woman extended her hand.

"I'm Madeline Kaiser," she said. "Andy Povitch is my colleague at Taft University. We have adjoining offices."

"I'm Nell Bane, but I don't think ... Dr. Povitch doesn't know me and..."

This woman—Madeline Kaiser—shrugged as if to say, please yourself, but she continued pleasantly, "Is this the first Shilliday Christmas party you've attended?"

"It is," replied Nell, her eyes still on the man identified as Andrew Povitch. Then, feeling like some further explanation was called for, she continued vaguely, "I am doing some research for Angela Shilliday."

This comment earned a raised eyebrow from Madeline Kaiser and the comment "Oh" that had an odd emphasis laid upon it.

Nell turned to give this woman a closer, keener look.

But Madeline Kaiser merely turned again toward the table where Povitch was now smearing mustard onto his ham.

"I could tell you quite a bit about Andrew Povitch," she said.

Now Nell addressed Madeline Kaiser directly.

"I think I would be very interested in what you have to say."

Nell Bane was a ghostwriter. She made it her business to dig up fact, innuendo, rumor and scandal, and to use what information suited her purpose, and she wasn't the woman to turn her back on any information offered.

"Let us," she said, "repair to a quieter corner of this party and speak further of these things."

Madeline Kaiser's smile took one corner of her mouth and tucked it up engagingly.

But there was a sudden stir among the guests. People shuffled toward the front staircase where two little girls were descending with their nanny. They wore matching white nightgowns with lace-edged hems that just brushed their bunny slippers. Sighs of "Adorable" and "How darling" went through the room like wind on a summer night as the little Shilliday daughters—Belinda and Bianca—were guided down the stairs by Glorimar. Nell figured that Glorimar had just finished tying the fresh satin ribbons in the silky blonde hair in order to make the appearance Angela Shilliday must have choreographed.

The little girls were well coached. Hand in hand, they scampered toward Dr. Thomas Shilliday, and with cries of "Grampy," they stretched prettily on tiptoe to kiss the patriarch. Then, like two tiny Wendys, they flew to their grandmother, aunties and father. They accepted compliments from the guests and sweetly answered questions about what they wanted Santa to bring them for Christmas. Finally the doting mother— Angela—stepped forward to bestow ostentatiously maternal kisses on her children and to direct Glorimar to lead the girls upstairs.

"Little Christmas angels," a guest was heard to say as the party-goers turned back to their drinks. And to conversation was soon roaring even louder than before.

"So what is it you want to know about Andrew?" Madeline Kaiser asked Nell.

Nell was careful.

"Well, he's a man of some fame now, isn't he? I am writing an article on the effects the Nobel Prize has on recipients. If there is something you could tell me, from your own observations, I'd be very interested to hear."

Nell's new companion took a card from her tiny evening purse.

"Give me a call, why don't you? This is a lousy place to carry on a conversation."

"Thank you. I will do that."

And Madeline Kaiser, responding to a tap on her arm from a man Nell did not know, turned away.

Good. Now Nell that could identify Andrew Povitch, she could watch him surreptitiously. She looked with distaste at the glass cup in her hand and was looking for a place to hide it, when instead she found herself being drawn into the hall by a man with a beard who wanted her opinion of a portrait hanging on the wall.

Nell milled on. She introduced herself to people and chatted away in the small talk language of conviviality. But she chatted with diffused attention, keeping an eye on Povitch. And she began to form opinions.

"Good evening. We've haven't met, but I've been admiring your dress. Very pretty indeed."

It was Beth Shilliday, Angela's charming mother-in-law, and Nell was pleased to be addressed. Also glad to be holding the cup, although the Glogg was hardly touched.

"I'm Nell Bane. And I know you are the creator of this marvelous Glogg."

The woman laughed. "Once a year. That's enough, don't you think?" she added conspiratorially.

That was a not question Nell wished to answer.

"What do you do?" asked Beth Shilliday, mercifully changing the subject."

"I'm a writer."

"Oh, like Angela."

"Yes," Nell replied. "Like Angela."

"And speaking of Angela," said Beth, "I'm sort of on duty. I promised to keep the dining table supplied with everything it needs. Lovely to have met you."

She squeezed Nell's forearm and melted into the crowd. Very physical people, these Shillidays, Nell told herself, resuming her Povitch reconnaissance.

Dr. Andrew Povitch had seemed to identify every young and pretty woman at the gathering, and had made it his business to seek introductions and smilingly chat each one up. The women of the moment, whom Povitch had cut from the covey, seemed completely charmed and very pleased to be wooed by this witty man and in very little time were dimpling and laughing.

A woman completely unknown to Nell but with an air of authority that said she wasn't used to being told no, demanded that Nell accompany her to see the marvelous draperies in the master bedroom. And indeed, guests were going up and down the stairs as if on an escalator. Nothing in the Shilliday house seemed to be off limits this night, and the party rampaged on all levels. So Nell was borne along to the master bedroom where she examined the window treatment and tried to comment learnedly. But when she finally escaped to the first floor, Andrew Povitch had disappeared.

In the dining room, though, she spotted him again. This time he was chatting up Julia Shilliday. In fact, he had her backed against the wall and more or less pinned there by a straight arm. Povitch was smiling seductively and Julia Shilliday was obviously enchanted. People squeezed past them on their way to the dining table and to the bar, but the couple didn't appear to notice as they gazed intently into each other's eyes.

Nell was tired of holding the sticky punch cup. At some point she had wrapped a cocktail napkin around the bottom to act as a coaster and now this napkin was stuck with the glue of Beth's amazing Glogg. Looking for a spot to ditch the cup, and not seeing any appropriate place, Nell made her way to the kitchen to put it in the sink and to rinse her sticky fingers. At the sink, however, she had an embarrassing encounter. Angela Shilliday had shanghaied her husband into the pantry and was giving him hell. Quietly, but clearly giving him hell.

"Get your damned sister away from him!" Angela demanded.

Tim Shilliday's response was muffled.

"I mean it!" Angela hissed. "And now! If you don't break it up I'm going to create such a scene..."

Nell fled.

In fact, she decided, it was time to find her coat. Passing through the dining room, she saw that Dr. Andrew Povitch and Julia Shilliday were still an item—and apparently a hot one.

If the promised scene were to follow, Nell didn't want to be around to see it.

Chapter 13

Nell had no opportunity to see Angela Shilliday after the Christmas party. Angela explained that she was far too busy with holiday commitments to handle the Povitch book too, and she was sure that Nell could carry on without her.

So Nell carried on.

She downloaded tutorials on ecological economics and dozed over back copies of *The ISEE Journal*. She even studied listings of conferences, looking for mention of Povitch's name or work. She revised the manuscript. Finally, she declared there was nothing more to do until she could pin Angela down.

She did telephone Madeline Kaiser, however, and they made a date to meet right after New Year's.

"I think it might be awkward to meet in my office at Taft," Madeline had told her. "Do you think you could meet me at home? I have a condo in Bay Village."

Nell had said that would be just fine. And she settled down to making her own holiday plans.

She invited Robert and Jerry—and of course, Bunty—to

Christmas Eve supper, and included the Fitzmaurices and a young couple from across the street who had just moved from California and who were starting their first New England winter. Then, on a whim, she invited Madeline Kaiser.

"Acting on the advice to never stifle a good impulse," Nell said, on the phone, "I'm inviting you to a soup supper on Christmas Eve. Just a few friends and those who wish can attend the candlelight service at First Parish over in Newbury. Box pews, carols, a walk through the snow-swept, lighted streets—everything Hollywood thinks a New England Christmas should look like. Friends are driving up from Beacon Hill, and I'm sure Robert would be pleased to chauffer you along. Please come—that is, if you're not doing anything special."

Madeline wasn't. And she seemed delighted to have a Christmas Eve plan.

So there would be soup, of course. Three varieties. Nell hauled out two more antique tureens from her collection and mused over soup recipes. Oyster stew, naturally, that old standard was expected. And she'd make Chicken Velvet Soup, a Christmas Eve recipe she'd inherited from her mother and that was only made at Christmastime, for it was sinfully rich and Nell was mindful of friends on Lipitor. And as a sturdy alternative to the cream soups, good old lentil sausage.

The little group had Christmas music on the Bose and drinks in hand when the Boston contingent arrived, Robert with snowflakes on his black topcoat and Jerry with arms piled with exquisitely wrapped gifts. A smiling Madeline Kaiser was introduced to everyone and she and Bunty made an almost instant connection through a friend they had in common.

Soon the dining room sideboard held three steaming tureens and stacks of bowls so guests could ladle the soup of choice.

"What charming bowls!" Madeline Kaiser exclaimed.

"Yes," Nell agreed, "They're Bunty's. She is a potter and has made quite a reputation for herself around Newburyport and the North Shore."

"I am impressed," Madeline said. "Pottery is one of my weaknesses. I wonder, Bunty, if you could tell me where I'd find some bowls of my own to purchase."

"This evening is so welcome," said Ann Fitzmaurice. "And so peaceful. Tomorrow Franklin and I will be with the grandchildren and it will be beautiful pandemonium—and we love it—but this is magical. Tonight, all is calm and all is bright."

Soup bowls in hand, the guests continued to mingle and talk until Franklin Fitzmaurice declared it was time to board the automobiles if they expected to get seats in First Parish. There were rustles and flourishes then as people found coats and decided on who would drive with whom.

"Remember to come back after the service," Nell called. "We'll have a wee dram before the fire and wish each other Merry Christmas."

CHICKEN VELVET SOUP
(A Christmas Eve Tradition)

6 tablespoons of butter
1/3 cup of flour
1/2 cup of milk
1/2 cup of light cream
3 cups of chicken stock or broth
1 cup of finely chopped chicken

1 large jar of roasted red peppers, drained and blotted dry with paper towels

Nell had tripled the recipe to serve the guests she was expecting and prepared the chicken a day before the party. On Christmas Eve she made a roux of the butter and flour, then stirred in the chicken stock, and while the guests were enjoying cocktails, she gently added the milk and cream, then the chicken. When the piping hot soup was swimming in the tureen, she floated stars cut from red peppers on the top and sprinkled minced parsley for a festive red and green, Christmasy presentation.

Yes, the evening had been a success, Nell decided, reviewing her Christmas Eve party. And instead of a carol, she hummed softly to herself as she gathered the soup bowls and fed them into the dishwasher.

"Soup of the evening", she sang to herself, *"beautiful sou-oop, Beautiful sou-oop, bee-u-tiful sou-oop."*

Chapter 14

Nell parked under the Common and marched south on Charles Street. There was a tricky moment at Tremont where she had to jump back onto the curb to avoid being mowed down by a careening cab. But, alive and uninjured—surprisingly—she continued down Charles, turned right on Fayette Street and entered the magical time warp of Bay Village where the sidewalks were corridors between the street cobbles and townhouse. Instead of stoops, stairs were carved directly into the buildings.

Nell found the address and was admitted to Madeline's tiny condo.

"This place is as small as a doll's house," Madeline apologized as Nell squirmed out of her coat in a foyer the size of a lavatory. "It's really just a tiny box."

"A candy box, though," Nell declared, looking around. "One of those perfectly designed ones with each exquisite chocolate tucked in its own ruffled cup."

The place did have an immediate charm comprised of

colors and light and the delicate scent of... thyme, was it? Lavender? Madeline's taste was perfect, and Nell gazed about with satisfaction.

The living room opened off the foyer and its windows faced the street. Window boxes at this season still held pine branches and ivy punctuated with unexpected remnants of driftwood.

"Why it even has a fireplace," Nell exclaimed, stepping into the living room. "Perfect!"

Madeline was gratified by her guest's delight.

"Tea? I have lapsang souchong or herbal, if you'd prefer."

"I haven't had a strong cup of lapsang souchong since Noah stepped out of the Ark," Nell declared. "Sounds like the very thing."

And soon they were seated on either side of Madeline's gently burning fireplace with hot cups of the smoky tea.

"I want to know more about Andrew Povitch," Nell began. "I'm helping Angela Shilliday write his biography, although I think I'm not supposed to admit that. I'm a ghostwriter, you see, and in this case, the client is keeping the ghost in the closet."

Madeline raised both eyebrows.

The eyebrow action was not lost on Nell.

"Do you know Angela Shilliday?" she asked.

"Of course. The economics department at Taft isn't overly large and Angela would be difficult to miss."

Nell waited.

After a sip of tea, Madeline continued.

"Angela did her undergraduate work at Taft. Then she began her graduate studies. She was away for a while but she returned not long ago to finish up and to work on her doctorate. I believe she's almost through—as soon as she finishes her thesis, that is."

Madeline Kaiser's smile was catlike. Or perhaps catty. Nell

wasn't certain which, but her mission today was to winkle out every shred of information on Andrew Povitch that Madeline Kaiser was able to give. Or was willing to.

"What can you tell me about Dr. Povitch?" she asked.

"It is a privilege to know Andy," Madeline began. "He's quite a fellow, and we've been friends for years. We met ages ago as undergraduates at Ohio State, lost touch, then surfaced at the same university—Penn State—when we were both on the faculty. Of course, Andy has traveled around far more than I. And has seen and done far more wonderful things. After Pennsylvania, I was happy to come to Taft and settle down in Boston. And then one day," she laughed, remembering, "into my cubicle of an office walked Andy Povitch. It was like a letter from home. Our offices have been side-by-side since. I've had a ring-side seat to his growing fame, and I've cheered him on with each new triumph."

A log in the fire descended, flinging sparks, and Madeline rose and used a poker to restore order in the fireplace.

"Andy is a charismatic man," she observed dispassionately. "You may have noticed that at the Christmas party."

Nell nodded. "I certainly did."

"He is very attractive and that may be his Achilles heel," Madeline continued. "His one fatal flaw. He is a womanizer, Andrew, and a skillful one. But it's not all on Andy's end. There is something about him that's like catnip to women. I've seen otherwise sound and sane women—*married* woman some of them—swoon when he walks in the room. Yes, he's attractive, and that's been ramped up considerably by the Prize. Fame is a powerful aphrodisiac."

The two women gazed into the fire.

"Is Andrew Povitch married? Or was he ever?"

"Oh, yes. First to a hometown girl named Mira something. They had two children. Sadly their son died in an accident several years ago and there's a daughter who lives in Arizona somewhere. Andy sees very little of her, and as far as I know Mira Povitch returned to the Cleveland area after they were divorced. They were married about fourteen years, and Mira had to put up with quite a number of Andy's dalliances during that time."

"You said first. I take it there were other Mrs. Povitches?"

"Only one other. His second wife, Bonnie. Blonde, leggy. The marriage lasted four years, before the beauteous Bonnie found out about Andy's bit of stuff on the side. She walked out, and I'm not sure Andy even noticed she was gone. He is a parallel romancer, you see. Before he breaks up with a woman—and breaks her heart—he is already wooing a new sweetheart."

"He seems to have a fondness for type," Nell observed drily.

This made Madeline chuckle. "Oh yes. He likes them tall and lanky, as fit and high-strung as race horses. Prefers them blonde and young. Youngish, rather. He's bored by babies and he's no cradle-robber. Late twenties, early thirties is his age bracket of choice."

"How long does he seem to stick with the 'woman du jour'?"

"Depends. He was married to Bonnie for four years. Not counting Mira, the first wife, that's probably the record. But the thing is about a womanizer like Andrew, he likes to have more than one woman on the string at a time. He's monogamous for a while with the new woman, but then his head gets turned by a newer model and he takes up with her without bothering to trade in Woman Number One. As a result, there's usually some insanely upset, jealous woman calling the office incessantly or lurking in the hallway waiting to pounce on him."

Madeline shook her head, obviously remembering a few interesting adventures.

"It's never dull, I can tell you, being Andrew's office neighbor. I've had to talk more than one hysterical woman off the ledge when she's discovered Andrew has moved on."

Madeline Kaiser smiled at some internal recollection.

"He can't help himself, you see. Being attracted to women is as much a part of him as his appetite for lunch. But to give the devil his due, the situation can't be laid entirely at Andy's feet. For every woman he takes up with, five others are eating their hearts out and crying into their beer."

"Do you speak from experience?" Nell asked.

Madeline Kaiser chuckled. "I'm not Andy's type. You saw him in action at the Christmas party. His eye went to that lovely young thing in the tiny black dress the moment she breezed through the door."

"That lovely young thing is Angela's sister-in-law," Nell told her.

"Oops," said Madeline thoughtfully. "I think I smell trouble."

But she did not elaborate.

"So you and Povitch are just friends." Nell summarized.

"And colleagues. One of the proudest moments I've ever known was when the Nobel was announced. The call came through around 5:00AM. Andy said he was in the middle of a dream and thought the news from the committee member on the phone was a sequence in the dream. He had a hard time making out what was happening. I was the first call Andy himself made and he was already in the office when I got there. It was the only time I've had Champagne for breakfast."

Madeline chuckled.

"And has success changed our boy?" Nell inquired.

Madeline grew pensive. "I'd have to say of course, and

then I'd have to say no. That's curious, isn't it? Fame didn't turn his head, but it brought a lot more traffic and attention his way. He was so busy for a year, he didn't even have time to teach. Took a leave of absence just to be a Nobel Prize winner in economics. Of course a lot of attention came to Taft as well, and the university was terribly pleased and proud. The administration took full advantage of their borrowed fame, I can tell you."

She considered some more and Nell waited.

"But did it change Andy? Not really. Not that I could see. He is still madly enthusiastic about his field of economics. Still trying to blaze new trails. Still burning the candle at both ends and having the time of his life. I think he gets invited to better parties now. Probably has an easier time scoring adoring young women."

Madeline Kaiser chuckled.

"The tea has grown cold," she said suddenly. "Should I boil a fresh kettle and start a new pot?"

Nell used her cell phone to check the time.

"To be honest, I should get on my skates. I'd like to get back to the Common Garage and claim my car before it gets dark. And it gets dark so early this time of year. But I've enjoyed visiting and the lapsang souchong was a treat. And I am grateful for the background you've given me on Andrew Povitch. I've been finding work on this biography to be very difficult without some solid knowledge about the main character. So thank you on all counts."

"I wish you luck with your assignment," Madeline Kaiser said neutrally. "You can call on me anytime."

Chapter 15

As soon as she could score a date with Angela Shilliday, Nell was back in the third floor study. Stripped of its holiday finery, the elegant old house looked faded, Nell thought, and her client, sitting across the desk, looked tired.

"A good holiday?" Nell inquired.

Angela shrugged. "Pretty much. The kids both had ear infections which limited activities to an extent. I assume you spent your holiday working on the book?"

The assumption that she had no meaningful personal life and nothing better to do than grind away at Angela's assignment, slightly nettled Nell. However she elected to overlook the implications and her own ruffled feelings and get on with business. Reaching into her briefcase, she withdrew several printed chapters and presented them to Angela, who accepted them with the air of a teacher about to grade a stack of homework papers.

As Angela read, a vertical line between her eyebrows deepened.

Finally she shook her head and removed her glasses.

"This won't do at all. For one thing, you are starting the book with the announcement of the prize. With the phone call Andrew got from the committee. I don't think that's the right place to start. And where did you get that information about the call from the committee? I didn't tell you that."

"I researched it," Nell told her. "I unearthed it."

She didn't mention the collaboration with Madeline Kaiser. Research was research, Nell reasoned silently, and not all research came from books. Besides, she knew Madeline was a reliable source.

But with the remark "Humph," Angela let the matter drop.

"Well, that's a detail," she remarked. "We'll deal with that later. The thing that I'm seeing though—and that really bothers me more at this point—is your writing style."

Nell stared.

"What on earth is the matter with it?"

"Well, it's different than mine," Angela pointed out. "This has to read like my writing. It has to sound like me. You'll simply have to rewrite this."

Nell sat quietly for several seconds.

"I would find it very difficult to compromise my writing style to that extent," she said. "You had an ample opportunity to evaluate my style before hiring me and you said nothing then. In fact, you seemed impressed. The reason people hire professional ghostwriters is to obtain a professional product. We all learn to write, but not everyone who can hold a pencil can be a writer. Now I will be happy to revise, but not to 'write down'. I hope you can understand that."

Angela Shilliday looked unhappy. She toyed with the paper clip that had held the papers together.

Nell watched.

"Why is it important to you," she asked gently, "to change

the style of the work we've done so far?"

The immediate answer seemed to involve the paper clip. Angela was apparently paying more attention to its complexities than to Nell's question. Finally she looked up and looked directly at Nell. There was a measure of defiance in her expression.

"Well, there's more to this project than Dr. Povitch's biography," she said.

Nell waited.

"I've gotten permission to use the biography as my thesis. For my doctorate. It took some persuasion, I can tell you, but I finally convinced my advisor to take it to the committee and after some nonsense, they gave permission. But the thing is, there's this deadline. It's like—essentially yesterday—so we've really got to stoke the fires and get up the steam."

Nell was staggered.

When she could speak again, all she could think to say was, "Your thesis. I had no idea. Why didn't you make this clear this before we started the project?"

Angela's answer was a shrug. "I didn't see that it was important at that point. Why? What's the big deal?"

Nell shook her head as if that would help her think more clearly. And it wasn't much help.

"Well, a thesis is a very personal thing. It's supposed to be your original work, isn't it?"

"Oh, it will be," Angela asserted. "You're just helping out is all. Everyone hires researchers. Assistants. That sort of thing."

She aimed a squint-eyed look at Nell.

"Besides, we've come too far for you to back out now."

Chapter 16

"I'm in the soup again, Robert," Nell sighed.

"Oh? All is not well in Shilliday-land?" inquired Robert Hutchins.

Was that just a tinge of ironic humor in his tone, Nell wondered.

"I'm not sure, Robert," she continued. "Maybe it's just me being me. May I bounce an ethical issue off you?"

"Certainly, my dear," Robert said generously. "My hide is Teflon. Bounce away."

"Well, I was working with Angela—and by the way, she was very picky about the draft! She didn't like my writing style. Said it wasn't enough like hers! Robert! I've read her early draft of the Povitch book and she's barely literate. It was like a pro shortstop being criticized by a Little Leaguer."

"Do you remember that Broadway song 'Everybody wants to be an art di-rect-tor'? Well, everyone thinks they're a writer."

"It is very hard to write," Nell sighed, "with someone hanging off the end of your pencil."

"True. But what's the problem?"

"It turns out that Angela has wangled a deal with the economics department of Taft. Not only does this book aim to be a best seller on the popular market, but it will also do double duty as her doctoral thesis."

"And?"

"*And?* That's all you're going to say? That isn't ethical, is it Robert, to have someone else write your thesis?"

"No," Robert's tone was measured, "it probably isn't. But it *is* done. I'm sorry to have to say it, because I don't believe it is strictly ethical, but there are ghostwriters out there who make very decent livings writing term papers and even doctoral theses for other people. Check the web. You'll see. Some of the good ones will even do the research for you."

Nell was horrified. And she was angry.

"Well, I don't think it's ethical," she shot back. "And furthermore, if Angela Shilliday had told me right up front that her intention was to use this book as a thesis as well as a simple biography, I wouldn't have accepted the job. I think she was deceitful and that certainly is an ethical violation!"

Robert waited for several moments to give Nell the chance to cool down.

Then he asked the question, "So what are you going to do?"

"Sputter!" Nell answered promptly. "And I'm going to consider my options. But first I'm going to sputter!"

Chapter 17

"Uh-oh," said Bunty, casting a suspicious eye at the clutter in Nell's kitchen. "I see all the signs of a ghostwriter escaping into soup-making. Dare I ask what's going on?"

"I'm sputtering," Nell told her neighbor. "Bunty, is this just me? I'll tell you a story and you tell me if I'm crazy."

"Ah. I can run from psychotherapy," Bunty pretended to be glum, "but I can't hide, is that it? But I'm too nosey to leave now. Tell."

So Nell told. She told how Angela was keeping her away from direct contact with the very person she needed to write about—Andrew Povitch. She told how Angela's contract with a ghostwriter was being kept hush-hush. ("She obviously thinks there's something ...well ... not quite up-and-up about the arrangement."). And finally she told how Angela had broken the news that the Povitch biography was also going to be submitted as her doctoral thesis.

"Robert says that hiring a ghost to write a thesis is a fairly common practice— and that may be—but it goes against my grain," Nell concluded truculently. "And I don't believe it's condoned by the universities and colleges either. If they did approve the practice, wouldn't they be handing out doctorates to every hack writer who concocts a presence on the web?"

But Bunty was more interested in Angela Shilliday herself than in passing judgment on the ethics of ghostwriting.

"What's she like?" Bunty wanted to know.

So Nell opened the refrigerator, took out an opened bottle of Shiraz, poured two glasses and prepared to answer.

"She's quite striking," Nell said, collecting her thoughts. "Tall, not pretty exactly but attractive. She'd turn heads walking through a restaurant. She knows how to dress and how to move. Excellent posture and marvelous poise. She seems very sure of herself and she radiates self confidence."

Bunty nodded encouragingly, so Nell thought some more, then continued.

"If you wanted to describe a woman who has everything, you'd just have to say 'Angela Shilliday'. Handsome husband who's a physician—a cardiologist with an impressive reputation. So there's money there. The family isn't wanting for material assets. So there's prestige and all the perks like the expensive country club and the professionally decorated house in Winchester. Two adorable little girls. You should have seen them at Angela's Christmas party, Bunty. Both in white nightgowns dripping with old-fashioned lace. They were costumed to look exactly like Clara in the Nutcracker and cued to come downstairs at the exactly the perfect moment."

Bunty grinned at the picture Nell was shaping.

"And she's bright, Angela," Nell went on.

She went to the Aga and gave the soup a vicious turn with the spoon. "I don't mean brilliant—just street smart and able enough to give the illusion of competence. I've read her writing though and it's pedestrian at best. The thoughts aren't original;

she just parrots back other people's ideas and the writing itself is only marginal. But with all of those drawbacks, she has still sailed to the head of the class."

"And where is she going, do you think?" Bunty's question was the first time she'd spoken. "What is it wants?"

"Wants?" Nell repeated. "Why, Angela wants it all."

CREAMY LEEK AND MUSHROOM SOUP

4 tablespoons of butter
1 pound of leeks, white part only—finely sliced
1/2 pound of mushrooms, roughly chopped
3 cups of vegetable stock
1 cup of milk
1/2 pound of potatoes, peeled and chopped into a small, even dice
3 ounce of Stilton cheese
Garnish:
4 tablespoons of horseradish
1 finely chopped gherkin pickle
4 tablespoons of sour cream
Minced parsley
Mix garnish ingredients together and chill

To make the soup, Nell melted the butter in a large saucepan and began to sauté the leeks and mushrooms. She cooked them gently for 10 minutes, thinking about Angela while she stirred. Then she added the vegetable stock, the milk, and potatoes and brought them to a boil before reducing the heat and simmering the soup until the potatoes were tender. When the soup was ready to serve, Nell crumbled in the Stilton cheese and ladled the soup into Bunty's bowls. A big dollop of sour cream-pickle-horseradish mixture went on top, and finally, a sprinkling of minced parsley.

Chapter 18

Nell beavered on with the Povitch biography, examining photographs, referring to books and papers the economist had published, and studying biographical materials harvested from any source she could find. There were a couple valuable accounts of Povitch winning the Nobel Prize for economics, including some good quotes from Povitch himself about his reaction to the phone call from the committee. And slowly, slowly, Nell made her way along, and the stack of pages grew as the printer chuntered out the words Nell typed into the computer.

Then Nell had an idea.

"Brilliant!" she said aloud. Then muttered, "Smarter than the average ghost."

And acting on her brilliance, she called Madeline Kaiser. Would there be any chance, she wanted to know, that Andrew Povitch might be lecturing at Taft? Perhaps giving a special speech or simply lecturing to a regular class?

There was.

Angela could have kissed Madeline.

"Madeline, do you think it would be possible to sneak me into a lecture?"

"What, sneak?" said Madeline Kaiser. "I'll set it up for you to audit a class. You can judge the great man for yourself."

Madeline had even been kind enough to check Angela Shilliday's class schedule to make certain Nell wouldn't run into her client in the halls of the economics department.

And so there was Nell Bane, feeling oddly nervous and a little furtive, attending her first college class in economics. She confessed her nervousness to Madeline.

"Why?" her friend wanted to know. "You're just going to sit at the back and gather impressions. You're not going to have to participate in a discussion or take a test."

But then Madeline had gone the second mile and had accompanied Nell right into the lecture hall and taken the adjoining seat at the back. Andrew Povitch had glanced up at them as they'd come silently in. When he recognized Madeline Kaiser, though, he gave her a conspiratorial grin.

When Povitch smiled, a quick-silver change transformed him to an engaging, almost-handsome man. Nell very rapidly lost her self-consciousness. She became completely absorbed in what Povitch was saying. He could have been speaking Slovenian, and Nell still would have been transfixed.

Andrew Povitch walked around as he spoke. He made eye contact with students, asked them questions, drew them into conversation as gracefully as he had chatted with guests at Angela Shilliday's party. The people in the crowded lecture hall were at ease and enjoying themselves. They laughed easily, asked questions eagerly, and exchanged banter with the professor, completely absorbed by this Svengali of ecological economics.

Nell found herself trying to deconstruct Dr. Andrew

Povitch's powerful magnetism. How, she marveled, could he make ecological economics at once understandable and exciting?

At the conclusion of the hour there was a spontaneous outbreak of applause that made Povitch laugh and doff an imaginary hat in thanks. A clutch of students rushed him before he could escape the podium, and Povitch was generous with his answers to their questions.

"Well," said Madeline, "what did you think?"

"Oh my," replied Nell, "it was wonderful. *He* was wonderful. I had no idea. And thank you so much, Madeline. Now that I've had the opportunity—*finally*—to see what all the fuss is about, it will make it so much easier to write what I have to."

"Would you like to meet him? I'd be delighted to introduce you."

Now Nell was like a shy high school girl.

"Oh, I shouldn't. Angela wouldn't like it."

Madeline scoffed. "Angela! Did you always refrain from doing everything your mother told you not to do? Didn't you ever run off the rails? Go out beer drinking when you were underage? Go skinny-dipping in the quarry that was off-limits? Angela Shilliday is your client, she isn't your keeper."

Nell felt that Madeline was throwing down a dare. And indeed, Madeline's merry brown eyes were full of amusement and challenge. Nell glanced back over her shoulder at Andrew Povitch who seemed ready, at last, to leave the lecture hall. She decided quickly.

"Okay. Alright. I'll do it!"

Madeline's laugh was triumphant and she took Nell's elbow in a proprietary way, calling as they went down the risers to the front of the hall, "Just a second, Andy. There's someone I want you to meet."

Nell was under no illusion that she was the sort of woman Andrew Povitch was dying to meet. After all, she was no statuesque, twenty-something blonde; she was merely a petite woman in late middle-age with softly graying hair. Oh, pleasant enough, and not unattractive—given who she was anyhow. But when Andrew Povitch took her right hand in both of his and leaned slightly toward her saying, "How very nice to meet you, Nell. Have you known my good friend Madeline for a long while?" she felt a current pass from his two warm hands right up her arm. For a second she was disoriented.

"Our friendship is rather new, actually," she told him. "But I think we may have been old souls together. Ours seems to be one of those relationships that doesn't require a long learning curve. Have you ever experienced something like that?"

This brought more than a chuckle from the famous man. In fact, Andrew Povitch laughed heartily. And wonderfully. He threw back his head and his laugh boomed.

"I have!" he declared. "I have indeed. Now, Nell, did you enjoy my lecture? Are you a student of ecological economics?"

"I've done a bit of reading on the subject," Nell answered honestly, but humbly. "But I certainly can't claim to be a student."

Madeline Kaiser, bless her, entered the conversation smoothly, using a gentle sort of verbal aikido to turn it to topics more comfortable for Nell.

"Nell lives in Newburyport, Andy, in this most perfect antique cottage. It has a fireplace so big you could set up housekeeping in it."

Povitch turned to examine Nell again.

"That's marvelous! How fortunate you are. Now, Nell, what is it you do in this antique house in Newburyport?"

The question was unexpected but one that Nell was accustomed to fielding. She had her standard answer ready.

"I write. I write things for money."

This brought a fresh crack of laughter from Povitch.

"That's delightful. And what is it you write in order to earn this money?"

"I'm a ghostwriter," Nell admitted honestly. "I write whatever my client is willing to pay for, and I've written just about everything except poetry and pornography."

A slender young man had been standing near the podium—politely and just to the side so as not to appear to be eavesdropping—but obviously attempting to engage the attention of Andrew Povitch. The young man made his move now with a raised forefinger.

"Dr. Povitch ... Sir ... I'm told there's a telephone call for you. The one you've been expecting, I believe ..." His voice trailed off.

"Ha!" cried Povitch. "Yes, indeed."

Then turning quickly to the women, he made his excuses.

"I must rush ..." His eyes returned to Nell. "I hope to see you again soon, however. I'd very much like to know more about your ghostwriting."

And he was off; the slender young man trailing after.

"Goodness," Nell exhaled. "A couple of close calls there, I think, but Madeline! He is everything you've said—powerfully charismatic. No wonder he breaks hearts. If I were thirty years younger, I might get in line."

"Thirty years younger and a foot taller," Madeline said sarcastically. "Then maybe you'd stand a chance with Andy Povitch."

Chapter 19

Once again, Nell found herself cooling her heels in Angela Shilliday's third floor study.

"Go on up," Angela had said, opening the front door. "I'll be right up. I just have to finish something."

"And hello to you too," Nell murmured under her breath, making her way up the front stairs.

And now it had been—what?—ten minutes? Maybe even fifteen. Nell, with the manuscript spread before her, was about ready to fold her cards and sweep out, when she heard running feet on the back stairs and Angela blew into the room.

"I really don't have as much time today as I'd thought," she said. "In fact, I've a migraine coming on. I've just had some bad news—some really lousy news."

Angela did look a little green, Nell thought. Not only that, she looked gaunt. Always smartly dressed, today she must have simply tossed on any old thing at hand—a cotton turtleneck with sprung cuffs and sweatpants that Nell would have described as "floods." Nell was surprised Angela even owned such tatty clothing.

Well, Nell had driven a ways to keep this appointment, but if Angela Shilliday were not well, she certainly couldn't argue or complain.

"Of course," she began shuffling the papers into an orderly stack. "You should go lie down at once. Take an asprin or ... whatever you take to help a migraine."

"Oh, leave those!" Angela directed. "I'll read the manuscript as soon as I'm feeling better."

And so Nell placed the neat stack on the edge of Angela's desk.

"I'll see myself out," she said. "Go. Go lie down."

Running lightly down the stairs, Nell encountered Glorimar dealing with the vacuum in the front hall. Glorimar gave Nell a rather glum look and shook her head.

"Angela isn't feeling well," Nell explained.

"Missus Shilliday isn't behaving very well either," Glorimar muttered.

"Oh dear," said Nell. "I hope everything improves soon."

So now, with the rug sort of pulled out from under the best part of the day, Nell tried to decide how to amuse herself. The weather was pleasant for a change so she decided to convince Bunty to meet her for lunch in Newburyport. She pulled out her cell phone and selected Bunty's number.

Chapter 20

There had been another accident on the MBTA. Nell looked up from her book to glance at the murmuring television. With some regularity, it seemed, someone was falling onto the train tracks these days. Usually the victim—either clumsy or drunk—had just stumbled or misjudged an edge, but lately there had been several vicious assaults. Innocent people had been intentionally shoved onto the track, often in advance of oncoming trains.

There was shocking footage of this assault, and Nell saw film of a young woman, not yet identified, being lifted unconscious onto the platform by a pair of struggling men. Passengers were reaching out to help, and there, indeed, was an Orange Line train that had mercifully been able to stop just short of the scene.

One of the rescuers, Nell learned, had suffered a broken arm in the effort and both Samaritans had cuts and bruises. But the victim—Nell saw a whoosh of blonde hair—had sustained serious injuries, including head trauma.

News microphones were eagerly shoved into the faces of several witnesses, and one woman was especially eager to describe what she'd seen.

'This man burst out of the crowd—just exploded out of nowhere!" Her arms flew wide as if to demonstrate. "We'd just heard the whistle of the inbound train from Oak Grove. And this young woman was standing near the platform's edge, close to that yellow painted line, because she was, you know, going to step into the train when it got there."

The eyewitness was excited.

"I'm still shaking!" she declared.

Another witness took up the story.

"The guy—the assailant," the man testifying seemed eager to use language appropriate to the event, "he rushed the girl the way a defensive tackle hits a receiver. *Pow! Wham!* She went right over the edge and he nearly went over right on top of her, that's how hard he hit. But he caught himself just in time and then he turned and pushed back through the crowd. Tried to make a dash for it."

The narrator paused for breath.

"Then these two other guys—they'd been waiting to get on the train—they raced after the perpetrator and caught him. The one guy was an off-duty cop and the other guy was built like a wrestler and he held the perp in a chokehold while the cop recited the Miranda. And the cop arrested him right there! Called a squad car while everybody's milling around and they hauled him away."

The witness shook his head. "Jesus, when you see something like that ..." He shook his head again.

Sirens wailing in the background added their bit to the drama.

Nell could hardly imagine it. To be standing there at Downtown Crossing—standing behind the yellow line, innocently minding your own business. A terrible thing to witness. A horrible thing to happen. She wondered if it were a random act by a crazed person or a dopehead. She couldn't imagine.

Chapter 21

Usually a news story like the attack on the subway dies quickly. It flares across the headlines for a day like a comet or a rare star while the news commentators goggle and murmur, but by the next morning, something new has happened and the story fades and winks out and you never hear what happens. Maybe you wonder for a while. But then you too, forget.

This story did not die however. The media kept nibbling at it as if it were a delectable treat, and one investigative reporter—a young woman called Tish Penney—sensing sensation, made it her business to follow the story even into the corridors of Mass General.

The identity of the young woman on the platform was revealed. She was Kirsten Wayborne, a graduate student at Taft University—a graduate student in economics.

Nell's attention was suddenly riveted.

The police were eager for Ms. Wayborne to regain consciousness so they could question her about the assault. From this information, Nell inferred that the police had determined the incident was not a random act but an event plotted and planned.

While the police detectives and Tish Penney—not to mention Nell Bane in her house in Newburyport—waited for Ms. Wayborne to come around, Nell called Madeline Kaiser.

Yes, Madeline knew Kirsten Wayborne. What would Nell like to know?

"On second thought," said Madeline, "why don't we just meet for lunch? The story could be longer than you think. And I know you'll find it interesting."

So Madeline and Nell met halfway between Boston and Newburyport—at a point they determined, after some discussion, to be Legal Seafoods in Danvers. They were shown to a very satisfactory back booth that afforded privacy as well as comfort.

Over glasses of sparkling water, Nell decided on grilled swordfish salad, and a cup of Legal's irresistible clam chowder while Madeline ordered a Maine crabmeat roll. Then Nell settled back to be told a story. As a storyteller herself, she loved hearing stories.

Madeline Kaiser helped herself to a roll from the basket, broke off a piece and buttered it liberally. She was enjoying her moment. Nell watched Madeline bite into the roll. A large bite. She watched Madeline chew. Slowly it dawned on Nell that her companion was drawing this thing out—tantalizing her on purpose.

"Okay," she said finally, "I know what you're doing. Stop teasing and tell."

"Haven't you wondered," Madeline began, "why this story about Kirsten Wayborne has not been shoved aside in favor of reports on the latest rape in Cambridge or the most recent stabbing in Roxbury?"

"Of course I've wondered. Even I realize there is a hook—

just one I haven't found yet."

"Kirsten Wayborne is not just a college student at Taft. She is also quite well connected to Boston legal circles. Her father is prosecuting attorney Anthony Wayborne, a partner in the august firm of Twine and Brown."

Nell's mouth drew into the shape of a silent "O", and she raised her eyebrows.

Madeline, watching for the reaction, smiled.

"And her mother," she continued, "is Probate Judge Catherine Lapp."

"Oh my."

"Oh my indeed."

"Do you know Kirsten?" Nell asked.

"I do," Madeline said. "She was a student of mine when she was an undergraduate, and a nicer girl would be difficult to find. Polite. Respectful. Whip-smart, and—may I add—very, very pretty."

Madeline paused and looked meaningfully at Nell, waiting for her to make the connection.

Realizing that something was expected of her, Nell was confused and thrown a little off base. Suddenly the tumblers clicked.

"Oh!" she exclaimed. "Oh my! Andrew Povitch."

Madeline Kaiser grinned.

"Exactly."

Chapter 22

Nell was pacing. The living room in the townhouse Robert Hutchins shared with his partner Jerry Gasso was small, and Nell could only manage seven strides before having to reverse direction. Robert, seated beside the fireplace, watched her.

"Stop," he said finally, "you're making me dizzy. What's going on with you?"

"Robert, do you know Anthony Wayborne?"

"Yes."

Nell stopped pacing and looked at him. The question had been a shot in the dark.

She waited.

"He was in my house at Harvard. Why do you ask?"

"Well, are you following the story of the young woman who was assaulted on the Orange Line in Downtown Crossing? The latest assault, I mean."

Robert nodded. "Yes, Anthony's daughter I'd guessed. Must be incredibly hard on Anthony and Catherine. And?"

Nell plopped down in the club chair across from Robert.

"Well, here's a laundry list of some bits of information I have. I am trying to puzzle them out and see if anything fits. And if anything *does* fit, I need to figure out where the puzzle pieces go."

Robert nodded his willingness to listen and help.

"Well, my client is Angela Shilliday. As you know. She is in the doctoral program at Taft University and has wangled a deal to write the authorized biography of Dr. Andrew Povitch. That's Fact One"

Nell held up a pinkie finger to illustrate Fact One.

"Facts Two, Three and Four."

One at a time, Nell displayed the next three fingers.

"Povitch is currently a member of the Taft faculty; he is an ecological economist, and just incidentally is a recent winner of the Nobel Prize for economics. Fact Five: Kirsten Wayborne is in the graduate program at Taft. Six: Economics is her field. Seven: she is a smashing-looking young woman. According to a reliable source—namely Madeline Kaiser, who is a long-time colleague and friend of Andrew Povitch—the good professor, also known as Randy Andy, has a jones for twenty-something, long-leggedity blondes. That's not really a fact—it's opinion. But this next *is* fact."

By now Nell's second hand had been conscripted into the count.

"Kirsten Wayborne has been the victim of a vicious assault—an assault intended to kill her; although she survived, she has very serious injuries. That was eight. Nine: The police suspect foul play. Ten: A felon called Digger Diaz was apprehended immediately in the T station. Eleven..."

Nell discovered she was out of fingers

"Well, eleven is Diaz is well known to the police but he's considered merely a small-time thug with no known reason to assault Kirsten Wayborne. Twelve: They, the police, believe the assault was not random. The source of the assault, in other word the brains behind Diaz, is not known."

Now Nell sat with all her fingers and both thumbs splayed in front of Robert Hutchins.

"And you want me to help you make the connections," Robert said. "In other words, help you solve the crime."

"Puzzle," Nell corrected. "I leave the criminal solutions to the professionals."

"Well, I'm glad to hear you say that," Robert said drily. "I hated to have to remind you that you are a ghostwriter not a crime-stopper."

He smiled gently at her. "But why do you care about this? It seems to me that you are only peripherally involved—or actually not involved at all. Is it just that maddening curiosity of yours coming out?"

Nell nodded miserably. "Maybe it is. But I just have a funny feeling, Robert. An ominous sense. I can't help but wonder if Angela Shilliday isn't somehow involved in this."

"You think Angela might have disguised herself as a co-assailant and pushed Kirsten Wayborne off the platform?" Robert chuckled.

"I know. It sounds mad, doesn't it?"

Chapter 23

After three days, Kirsten Wayborne regained consciousness and was able to submit to an interview by a police detective. Tish Penney's vigilance had paid off and she was able to spot the detective entering Kirsten's room in the company of a uniformed officer. Ms. Penney also had the triumph of being the first to reveal that Kirsten Wayborne, upon questioning, had told the police about several threatening emails she'd received in the past weeks.

No, she didn't recognize the sender. They were from some unknown person with a gmail account.

And no, she hadn't tried to send a response. The messages had upset her, but they hadn't really alarmed her. She'd just deleted them and tried to forget them.

The content in the emails was brief. Kirsten Wayborne was warned to stay away from Dr. Andrew Povitch. Tish Penney then furnished a brief description of just who this Dr. Povitch was, including the misinformation that he was an environmental economist.

Nell was nettled. Having taken some pains to educate herself to the fine distinctions between the disciplines of economics, she was disgusted when these distinctions were not correctly drawn.

Who, Nell wondered, was the mystery author of these emails?

Moreover she wondered if Povitch's connection with the Wayborne incident should be explored and included in the biography.

Well, that would be up to Angela Shilliday, of course, and Nell resolved to ask at their next meeting.

But before that meeting could take place, the vigilant Tish Penney flung some more facts at the citizens of Boston.

Digger Diaz had admitted to the assault—well, having been run down in the T station and put in a chokehold, how could he do anything else? According to Tish Penney, Diaz had sat right there in the police station and claimed he'd been hired by another felon—obviously one of a slightly higher rank and level of skill than Digger, who had displayed an inability to think and push at the same time. Marky Negolian, Diaz claimed, had paid him $300 to shove Kirsten Wayborne off the platform just ahead of the inbound train.

"Three hundred bucks?" The cop was incredulous. "You shmuck, Diaz! You risked life in the slammer for three-hundred lousy clams?"

"I needed the money," Digger Diaz had whined. "I hadda pay my rent, ya know, and my landlord was all over my back."

Marky Negolian, like Diaz, was well known to the police, and it was agreed that he was a slippery character as well as a sleazy one. He was brought in for questioning, but Marky Negolian was not as forthcoming as Digger Diaz. He had a chippy attitude and he admitted nothing. The only thing Negolian claimed was "that scumbag Diaz was a liar as well as a scumbag." And after several vigorous hours in the company of Marky Negolian, the cops agreed there were no grounds for holding him. Yet.

Tish Penney, however, was still logging long hours on the case, dividing her time between Mass General and police headquarters on New Sudbury Street. Then Kirsten Wayborne was released from the hospital to her parents' home, and Tish Penney was able to concentrate on current events in police headquarters on New Sudbury, where she was getting a lot of bad vending machine coffee and little else.

Chapter 24

Nell and Angela Shilliday were deep in the draft of Andrew Povitch's biography. Two heads, one dark brown, the other light, were bent to the business, and both women were wearing reading glass as they reviewed chapter twelve.

"I don't like this paragraph," Angela said. "Can you straighten it out?"

Nell took a look.

"Sure. That's easy. Just mark it for revision."

Angela's red pen scrawled "Rev" in the margin and she continued reading.

Nell watched her. No, Angela Shilliday definitely looked different. She seemed drawn; there was a gray look to her complexion—a complexion that had been quite rosy when they'd met in the fall. Nell wondered what had made the difference.

Angela sat back with a sigh.

"I guess that's it. Enough here to keep you busy for a while?"

"Quite busy," Nell replied. "But it's manageable. We're making good progress, you know. We should be wrapping this up soon. And what then? Do you have a publisher lined up?"

"Something'll open up, I guess." Angela's answer was laconic. "Some university press will probably be keen to publish. In fact, I expect there'll be a bidding war to get their hands on Andy Povitch's biography."

Nell felt this was unreasonably optimistic, but she refrained from saying so.

"Oh!" she suddenly exclaimed. "There is something I've wanted to ask you. This unfortunate incident that's happened to one of the students in your department at Taft. There was mention in the news that the young woman was warned to stay away from Andrew Povitch. I was just wondering if that should be included in the biography—you know, attractive, famous professor and social scientist..."

But Nell didn't have a chance to finish. Angela Shilliday's gray complexion turned white as marble, and she cut off Nell's with a chop of her hand as if she were about to break bricks.

"Absolutely not! That incident with Kirsten had nothing to do with Andy. *Has* nothing to do with him. It's completely outside the boundaries of this book!"

Feeling chastised, Nell could only apologize.

"Yes, I understand. I'm sorry I brought it up."

She removed her reading glasses and slid them into their case. Then she gathered the scattered papers of the manuscript and tapped them into alignment, fastening them with a clip.

Across the desk, Angela brooded darkly.

Nell waited, but Angela's mood hung between them like a sooty cloud, and she offered nothing more.

"I'll just see myself out," Nell suggested quietly.

She paused in the rec room to glance back into the study, but Angela had not moved.

Chapter 25

Angela Shilliday's dark mood was communicable. Nell had caught it. Recalling the morning's meeting on the long drive home to Newburyport, she brooded as Angela had done. She tried to deconstruct their conversation in the same manner she tried to figure out the ingredients of a dish tasted in a restaurant so she could repeat the recipe in her own kitchen. In college she'd been taught to explicate seventeenth century poetry, and now she picked at remembered bits of dialogue. Here a word, there an intonation... Nell shook her head. Angela's fierce reaction was one more addition to the series of small facts added to her growing collection of puzzle pieces.

"I'll have to take off my shoes," grumbled Nell, "and start ticking off these facts on my toes."

She wondered what Robert would make of this. Or Madeline Kaiser. Or her good neighbor Bunty Whitney. But this was Nell's problem and hers alone to puzzle out. She decided to employ her customary therapy—soup-making. But that too demanded thought. What could she make?

By the time Nell got to Scotland Road, she'd made her decision. Princess Diana's elegant watercress soup. She'd found the recipe in a back issue of *Life Magazine.* It enchanted her to imagine the glamorous princess standing in a kitchen, whipping up the soup. What did the kitchen look like? And for whom was she creating this delectable soup?

Nell pulled into Tendercrop Farm to buy the watercress.

PRINCESS DIANA'S WATERCRESS SOUP

2 tablespoons of butter
2 tablespoons of flour ounces
2 cups of chicken stock
12 ounces of watercress, chopped, with large stems removed
1 cup of light cream

After she'd converted the British measurements to American, Nell began to make the soup. She made a roux by heating the butter in a saucepan and stirring in the flour. She removed the pan from heat before pouring in the chicken stock and whisking hard. Next she brought the soup to a simmer and added watercress, covered the pan and let the soup steep slowly over very low heat for 20 minutes. Finally she plunged the immersion blender into the pot and when the soup was silk-smooth, she added the cream and heated the soup gently.

The therapy worked. She felt better. How could you be morose when consuming a bowl of Princess Diana's watercress soup?

Chapter 26

"Bunty, I need to get away for a bit. Get some fresh air up my nose and put other sights before my eyes. Do you feel like heading upcountry with me?"

But Bunty couldn't. A nephew's wife had broken her arm and Bunty had agreed to play caretaker while the nephew was at work.

"It means changing diapers," Bunty grumbled, "and driving Mary Claire to orthopedic appointments and then kicking my heels in waiting rooms. And you know what orthopedists' offices are like at this time of year," she demanded. "Full of broken wrists and misery. Full of flu germs too, now that I think of it."

"You're just aggrieved because you can't go batting off," Nell told her.

"Damn right!" Bunty shot back.

But Nell went right on. "You're good-hearted, Bunty, and you love Gregory and Mary Claire. Wild weasels couldn't tear you away if they needed you."

"Well," Bunty growled. "You have a good time even if I can't. And for God's sakes be careful driving."

Nell had thought about heading along the Maine coast, but at the last minute she turned inland and cruised up Route 89 to Vermont, dropping anchor at the spectacular Quechee Gorge. She booked herself into a small inn with a Jacuzzi right in her room, and she made a dinner reservation at Simon Pearce, where, in Nell's opinion, the dining room was just perfect! The hand-blown glass sparkled under track lighting and candle glow, and Nell was given a table with a view of the gorge and the falls. Her celebratory Martini arrived in a hefty, Simon Pearce signature glass that was frosted with cold. One drop of water had materialized out of the frost and traced its way down the side of the glass.

Nell decided on crispy roast duck with haricots verts, but for starters, she couldn't resist the famous Vermont cheddar soup. To her delight, the restaurant was generous about sharing its recipes, noting that the quantities were restaurant-size. That was fine with Nell. She tweaked the amounts and made the soup as soon as she'd returned to Newburyport. Then she summoned Bunty—and as a consolation prize—invited her to share a bowl. Bunty asked for seconds.

VERMONT CHEDDAR SOUP
A Famous Simon Pearce Recipe

1-1/2 quarts of water
1 clove of garlic, minced
6 tablespoons of flour
5 tablespoons of butter
1/2 of cup heavy cream
1 bay leaf
1/2 lb. Cabot Sharp Cheddar cheese, grated
1/2 cup carrots, grated

1/2 cup celery, minced
1 small onion, chopped
1 cup half & half
1 teaspoon fresh thyme, finely chopped
Salt & fresh ground pepper

Nell blanched the carrots and celery in boiling water, drained them and set them aside. She melted the butter in heavy stockpot and in it, sauted the onions and garlic, cooking them to softness. She added the flour to the butter/onion mixture and stirred to make a roux. Then, turning the heat on the Aga very low, she let this cook for 15 minutes, giving it a casual stirring every so often. Then it was time to add the boiling water, carefully, 1/3 at a time and whisking the mixture smooth after each addition.

Nell seasoned the soup with thyme, bay leaf, salt and pepper. She scraped the carrots and celery into the boiling water and cooked until they were just tender, drained them and added them to the stockpot along with the grated cheese. Finally, she stirred in the half and half and heavy cream, preparing to serve the soup hot but taking care not to overheat it.

Chapter 27

But all pleasant interludes end. And so they must, or they would cease to be pleasant interludes and simply become mundane routines, unnoticed and unappreciated. In due time, Nell found herself back in Angela's Shilliday's third floor study, seated on the guest side of the desk, contemplating the crown of Angela's bent head and the Elsa Dorfman photograph of the fabulous Shilliday family. On the floors below, the homely chores of the household were being carried on. Nell heard a vacuum cleaner huffing back and forth across carpeting. A bell rang and the vacuum ceased.

A few moments later, Glorimar—her eyes open wide—stood in the doorway.

"Missus Shilliday, there are some policemen downstairs to see you."

Nell had heard the cliché "eye-popping" many times, but for the first time, she actually saw it. Angela Shilliday's eye seemed to bug out of her head. She stared uncomprehendingly at Glorimar. Nell stared at Angela. It seemed that entire minutes were passing and all three women were frozen. In fact, Nell did feel a chill.

Then slowly, very slowly, Angela stood. She moved to the doorway and passed through it as though she were sleepwalking. Glorimar moved just slightly aside to allow her to pass.

Nell continued to sit, Glorimar continued to stand in the doorway, but their eyes met, and Nell knew her own eyes were as wide as Glorimar's and that her expression was similar—a combination of confusion, curiosity and controlled panic. There was no sound from below.

After an eternity, Nell broke the silence.

"Perhaps we should go down and see if ... see if she's alright?"

Glorimar nodded and Nell rose and followed her down the backstairs. Both women stepped silently, each placing a foot with care, tacitly unwilling to intrude with a creaking stair or a heavy tread. At the second floor, it was Nell's custom to move down the hall and use the wide front stairs to reach the first floor, but Glorimar indicated with a jerk of her head, that they should continue on the backstairs. Nell nodded. In the kitchen, they listened, but there was only silence. Nell, on tiptoe, followed Glorimar into the front hall.

Now they could hear Angela's voice coming from Tim Shilliday's study. She was on the phone. In the living room, two men were standing with their backs to the fireplace—one a uniformed cop and the other wearing a khaki overcoat.

Nell couldn't help flashing on Peter Falk's Columbo character.

Angela came out of the study, still wide-eyed and disheveled, like she'd been running her fingers through her hair. Seeing Glorimar and Nell, she appeared relieved.

"Oh!" Nell got the fleeting impression that she was editing

her explanation, making it plausible.

"I ... I find I have to go with these men to ... well, go with these men for a while."

The officers regarded Angela levelly. She addressed them.

"I couldn't reach my husband. He's in surgery, apparently. But I left word to have him call home as soon as ... soon."

She turned again to Nell and Glorimar, this time there was a pleading note in her voice.

"Can you stay here to take Dr. Shilliday's call when it comes? To tell him where I am?"

"Missus Shilliday," Glorimar said softly, "I have to pick up Bianca at pre-school."

"I'll do that," Nell volunteered quickly.

Glorimar turned to her, looking miserable.

"But you can't. You have to be checked out by the school. Have written permission. Only Dr. and Missus Shilliday and I are on the list."

"Oh, of course." Then Nell had another idea. "I'll stay here then. Wait for Dr. Shilliday's call and tell him ..."

Unsure, she turned to Angela, pleading silently for an explanation. But Angela Shilliday seemed as unprepared as Nell.

Peter Falk came to her aid.

"You'll be at Boston headquarters, ma'am. In Dorchester. I think you'll be there for a while and he can catch up with you there. He may want to contact your attorney."

Nell was numb, but Glorimar was perceptive and resourceful. She went swiftly to the hall closet and got Angela's coat. She wrapped it around her employer, adding a long scarf which she wound and tied expertly. She might have been dressing one of the little Shilliday girls. She added a pat on the shoulder, then a quick hug.

"You'll be fine, Missus Shilliday. Nell and I will see to the children and get the message to Dr. Shilliday. Don't you worry about a thing."

Angela Shilliday submitted to Glorimar's attentions as if she were a wooden doll. A cardboard cutout. Nell thought of adding a hug of her own, but she'd never hugged her client up to now, nor had she thought of it, and this didn't seem like the time to start hugging.

"Take care," she added now. "Don't worry."

"Don't worry!" she chided herself silently. "Of course she's going to worry."

But Nell wondered if Angela Shilliday knew what was happening.

The policeman and the detective left with her, hurrying to a squad car waiting at the curb. They seemed to take with them much of the oxygen in the room. An odd tension was lifted though, leaving a weird flatness. Once again Nell and Glorimar faced each other, mirroring each other's expression, this time puzzlement tempered with concern.

Glorimar looked at a clock.

"I've got to be in the car pool queue in ten minutes, and I can't dare be late. Will you be alright here?"

"Got to be," Nell replied, adding more heartily. "Of course! I'll wait right beside the phone in the study. Wait for Dr. Shilliday's call."

Glorimar nodded grimly and departed.

Nell waited. And waited some more. She examined the spines of the books in the study. What had she expected? Medical books? Thrillers from *The New York Times* book section? Biographies? But the bookshelves were tricked out with antique volumes purchased by some interior decorator bent on creating a stage set of erudition. Nell snorted in disgust. Books were meant to be read and reread. Cherished and dipped into when you wanted to read just that particular poem or remember how James Joyce had handled Molly Bloom's soliloquy or check the act where Banquo appears.

When the phone rang, she jumped.

"Angela?" Tim Shilliday's voice was anxious.

"No, it's ..."

"Where's Angela? I got an urgent message to call."

"It's Nell Bane, Dr. Shilliday. Your wife had to leave with ... well, she left with a policeman and a detective. They were heading for police headquarters in Boston, I believe—the main one in Dorchester."

The silence on the other end of the line, Nell took to be the silence of a man completely flabbergasted.

"I ... did she ...?"

"It was suggested," Nell said quietly, "that you might want to take an attorney when you see her."

Dr. Shilliday hung up with a clatter and without voicing the usual, polite farewells. Nell did not blame him.

Miss Bianca Shilliday, age four-and-a-half, strode into the kitchen wearing a backpack. Glorimar trailed her like a supernumerary carrying a large, warped-looking sheet of paper instead of a spear. The paper had obviously been quite wet recently but now was dry and featured wide swaths of tempera paint. Mainly orange and purple. Neither Nell nor Glorimar had any idea of what the images were supposed to represent, and neither would be so insensitive as to ask.

"I'm hungry," Bianca Shilliday announced, coming out of the straps of her backpack with a practiced series of shrugs and shiftings.

"Soup for lunch," Glorimar told her. "Coming right up."

"I want macaroni and cheese," the child said decisively. "The kind in the purple box. The Annie kind."

"This is not the day to argue," Glorimar murmured. She looked at Nell. "How 'bout you? You want to split a can of soup with me?"

Nell believed deeply in soup—even the canned kind. She believed in its powers to warm and soothe, to nourish and to heal. And truth to tell, she was feeling a bit dazed and wobbly from the events of the morning.

"I can't think of anything better," she told Glorimar sincerely.

Chapter 28

Full of wonder—and sadness, too—Nell wandered through the evening. The images kept haunting her, one after another like a slideshow. There was Angela Shilliday's marble face remembered. She'd obviously known something was up because she hadn't seemed all that surprised with Glorimar's announcement of the police downstairs. Stunned, yes, but not surprised. What, Nell wondered, did Angela know? Or what had she done?

Next came an image of Tim Shilliday. His shock and lack of comprehension when he'd spoken with Nell on the phone were genuine, Nell was sure of that. She tried to picture him arriving in Dorchester at the big station. Did he take her suggestion and bring his attorney? And what happened then? Were Tim and the attorney able to bring Angela home?

And who was at home? Glorimar was staying with the little girls, but what did Glorimar tell them when they wanted to know where mummy and daddy were?

By morning's light, wonder and sadness were giving over

to curiosity. Nell thought of telephoning the house in Winchester and trying to speak with Glorimar, but that seemed insensitive. So she brooded instead.

But somehow the news that Angela Shilliday had been transported by a detective to Boston Police Headquarters had filtered through the economics department of Taft University, and Madeline Kaiser reached out to Nell.

"I wonder if you heard," she said delicately, "that Angela Shilliday has been arrested."

"Arrested!" Nell was shocked. "No! I hadn't known she was arrested, but I did know she left her house with a pair of policemen. We were working on the book when they came to the house. She left with them but I didn't know why."

"Ah," Madeline said sagely, "so you did know something."

"Well, not about the arrested part. Can you tell me anything? I really have been worried. She left the house with the cops and all Glorimar and I could do was stand there with our mouths open and then hold the fort for the children. What on earth was she arrested for?"

Madeline's reportorial style was a masterpiece of unbiased oral journalism.

"Apparently Angela was the one sending threatening emails to Kirsten Wayborne."

"Angela!" Nell couldn't believe this. "Why would she do that?"

"Well," Madeline continued drily, "because she wanted Kirsten to break off her relationship with her professor, Dr. Andrew Povitch."

"Oooh," Nell breathed. Then she thought of something else. "But what business was it of Angela's?"

"Apparently Angela wanted Andy all for herself."

Nell was stunned. "You mean Angela and Andrew Povitch were having an affair?"

"I must say, Nell, you aren't very quick on the uptake, are you? You mean you didn't know that they were, as they used to say in the 'forties, a hot item?"

Nell was too shocked to be embarrassed.

"I did not! She never said!"

"Well, would she? But didn't you ever wonder how she knew Andy so well? How she snagged the plum job of writing his authorized biography?"

New emotions were beginning to surface within Nell as each revelation opened.

"Remember how I told you that Andy is something of a serial monogamist?" Madeline continued. "He woos a woman and when he wins her, he turns to the challenge and the excitement of a new conquest. The old doll just fades away. Evidently Kirsten Wayborne was the new conquest and Angela was the old one. Everyone in the department knew it. Everyone except Angela."

Madeline paused. Came up for air, Nell thought.

"When Angela found out about Kirsten, she was furious. Threw a blazing fit of temper right by the copier. I wasn't there but I heard about it later. Of course, most of the people standing around didn't get it right away that this scene had anything to do with Andy. Angela was always very circumspect."

"Madeline," Nell said now. "Where is Andrew Povitch now? What is he doing about this ... this unfortunate incident?"

Chapter 29

The editors must have felt the story was juicy enough to reward Tish Penney with a byline. And now Nell, having poured her morning coffee, poured over Tish Penney's words in the newspaper. The coffee cooled while, riveted, she read.

Doctor's Wife Stalks Nobel Prize Winner's Lover
By Tish Penney
Angela Shilliday, socialite wife of noted cardiologist Dr. Timothy Shilliday, was arrested yesterday in her home in Winchester and taken to Boston Police Headquarters for questioning. Shilliday stands accused of sending anonymous threatening emails to Kirsten Wayborne of Newton and for possible involvement in a plot to kill Wayborne by shoving her into the path of an MBTA train in Downtown Crossing.

Wayborne, although seriously injured in the assault, was saved from death by the quick action of two other passengers on the platform, as well as alert action on the part of the train driver who was able to halt the train just short of the accident scene. The assailant, Digger Diaz (among other aliases) was apprehended by two other passengers in the station, one of whom was off-duty policeman Sgt. Manuel Ramirez who read Diaz his Miranda rights before arresting him on the spot. Under questioning from police, Diaz admitted to accepting money to carry out the assault. The hunt for Diaz's accomplice led to Marky Negolian, a felon with a long rap sheet and well known to the police. Police were not able to immediately disprove Negolian's alibi.

Kirsten Wayborne is the daughter of Anthony Wayborne Esq., a prosecuting attorney with the legal firm of Twine & Brown, and Probate Judge Catherine Lapp.

"We are eager to see this very unfortunate matter resolved and brought to a just and satisfactory conclusion," commented Anthony Wayborne.

He refused to name the attorney who will be handling the case, but speculation has pointed to Justin Doan, Esq., a leading prosecutor at Twine & Brown.

Ms. Shilliday was arrested when emails to Wayborne were discovered on her office computer at Taft University, where Shilliday is a doctoral candidate and part-time instructor in the economics department and where Wayborne is a graduate student. Also in the Taft economics department is Dr. Andrew Povitch, a winner of the Nobel Prize for Economics. Shilliday's emails warned Wayborne, who is rumored to be in a relationship with Povitch, to stay away from the Nobel Prize-winning economist.

Although no one in the Taft economics department was willing to speak on the record, it is apparently common knowledge that Povitch and Shilliday are also in a relationship, although their affair is believed to be on the skids.

Under questioning, Ms. Shilliday at first admitted to an acquaintance with Negolian. She was advised, however, by Paul Burns Esq., an attorney for the Shilliday family, to make, no further comment until a defense attorney could be established. She *attempted to retract her earlier statement.*

The family has subsequently hired Attorney George Grenier, known as "The Grinder" for his ability to reduce witnesses for the prosecution to hamburger. There is some feeling in legal circles that the hiring of "The Grinder" is the next thing to an admission of guilt.

Shilliday was released on Friday on $10,000 bail and ordered not to leave her residence. In the meantime, Boston police detectives continue to explore Shilliday's connections—if any—to Marky Negolian and Digger Diaz.

Chapter 30

Robert Hutchins must have been reading the paper over coffee as well, for the phone rang just as Nell was carrying her mug to the sink to toss the cold dregs down the drain.

"I assume you've already looked at the paper," was Robert's dry greeting.

"I have," Nell said tiredly. "Oh, Robert, what's going to happen now?"

"Do you mean what's going to happen with Angela Shilliday? Or with the biography you and she are writing?"

"Both, I suppose. I am just too shocked to think."

But then Nell did have a thought.

"Robert! What if I've been consorting with a murderer?"

Robert made a small sound of amusement. "That doesn't make you an accessory to a crime. You have a writer's overly-active imagination, Nell. But I would think the writing project would be brought to a halt. And what concerns me is that your income will be halted too."

"I hadn't thought of that," Nell said slowly. "Oh dear. I've received a third of the fee and we were just at a point where I was going to declare the first draft of the manuscript finished and bill the second third. Rats!"

The archaic expression brought a chuckle from Robert.

"Well, we can't know what's going to happen," he said consolingly. "Let's just wait and see. This unpleasant matter might be just a huge misunderstanding and there will be apologies to the Shilliday family and the police will sort out the proper source of poor Kirsten Wayborne's assault."

"We can hope," Nell replied. But she had her doubts.

Doubts which seemed to be confirmed later in the morning with a call from Madeline Kaiser.

"We do live in interesting times," was Madeline's opening statement.

"Are you calling from Taft?" Nell wanted to know. "I've been imagining all morning what's been going on there."

Madeline grunted.

"Pretty much what you'd think: gossip, rumor, speculation, innuendo. Suddenly everybody knew or was suspecting something. The halls are fairly buzzing."

"Where is Andrew Povitch?"

"Not here," Madeline replied. "But he called me a half hour ago and invited me to lunch at the Harvest. Shall I give you a call later?"

"Oh, would you! I really am curious about Angela, and I'm also curious about the fate of the biography. Robert is counseling me to bide my time and saying that all will be revealed in the fullness of time. But biding my time is not a talent I've cultivated. I want immediate results. I want to know everything as soon as possible."

This brought a chuckle from Madeline Kaiser and the promise to scour out every fact she could.

Nell paced after she'd hung up the phone. Then, as a

distraction, she made some soup. A mindless sort of soup that involved opening a lot of cans.

AUTUMN BEAN SOUP

2 cans of cannelloni beans
1 can of red kidney beans
1 can of chickpeas
8 cups of chicken broth
2 large onions, chopped
1 Tbl. Spoon each of dried basil, oregano and parsley
1 package of fresh spinach, washed and torn into small pieces
1 cup of dry white wine
Parmesan cheese

Nell ground around the tops of the bean cans with a can opener, poured the beans into a colander in the sink and ran water over them to rinse them thoroughly. While the beans drained, she chopped the onions and melted them in a little olive oil in the soup pot. Then into the pot went the broth and beans. Nell brought the mixture to a simmer and let it bubble for a while. Then she pulled the pot off the stove. At suppertime, she would heat it, add the spinach, then the wine. And she'd serve it with plenty of Parmesan cheese.

And since there was enough soup in the pot to nourish a full family, she bottled up most of the soup and walked across the street to share with the young couple from California who would be returning at the end of the work day to a dark house and who would welcome a hot tureen of soup.

Chapter 31

True to her word, Madeline Kaiser got back in touch with Nell after her lunch with Andrew Povitch.

"You should know," Madeline said, "that I spilled the beans to Andy."

"Beans? What do you mean?"

"I let him know that Angela had hired a ghostwriter. That she wasn't really authoring his biography. I hope you're not angry that I did that," Madeline sounded contrite, "but I know he was counting on that biography, and I'm not at all sure that it will be written now."

Nell thought for a moment.

"It really doesn't matter to me that he knows," she said slowly. "It was Angela's secret to keep. Way back last fall I asked to meet Andrew Povitch and interview him for the book, which I felt I really needed to do. It was awkward to keep the subject you're writing about at such an arm's length. I mean, if he'd been dead or something, that would have been different, but he was totally accessible. But from her reaction, you'd have thought I'd asked to have him sire my child. My goodness." Nell, remembering, shook her head.

"I recall that," Madeline said. "You were finally allowed to come to that party and gaze at the great man from a distance. That's when we met."

They both laughed, remembering. In history's distance, the incident seemed absurd. But Nell came quickly back to the subject.

"So what did he say when you told him?"

"First he was sort of disbelieving. Then angry. There was a 'What was Angela playing at?' sort of moment. Then he began to see the humor in it all. He really has quite a good sense of humor, Andy."

"What did he have to say about the Kirsten Wayborne thing though? Was he shocked that Angela would do such a thing?"

"Well," said Madeline pragmatically, "I think we have to say alleged—*alleged* to have done such a thing. She's been arrested but she hasn't been convicted. Yet. But yes, he was shocked. And then...well, in a funny way I think he wasn't. I think Andy had begun to see a side of Angela Shilliday that was less than nice. She could be charming, but that charm was sort of digital. I mean she could turn it on and off with the flick of a switch."

"Does he think she did it? Arranged the hit, I mean."

"He didn't really say," Madeline said carefully. "I think he's worried for her. In fact, I know he is. He does care about her even though he was trying to break off the relationship."

"Did he say that? Break if off?"

"Not in those words. He was trying to let her down gently, I think. And like all of us, he is stunned, shocked, confused, and finding this whole thing terribly hard to believe. And finally, he is very concerned about Kirsten Wayborne. He talked quite a bit about her. She is doing better, apparently, and she is expected to make a full recovery. But heavens! What a terrible thing to go through!"

Nell murmured agreement. Then Madeline caught her off guard.

"He wants to see you."

"What?"

"Andy Povitch wants to meet you."

Chapter 32

The morning was exceptionally fine and Nell felt energized. On impulse, she decided to drive to Winchester. The need for a field trip compelled her, and besides, she'd been wanting to speak with Glorimar. Had wanted to talk with her but had been reluctant to call. On this fine morning, she decided to take the drive and the risk.

The charming house seemed ghostlike. "Like it's holding secrets," Nell thought privately.

"Now, you're indulging in anthropomorphism," she murmured to herself, deciding to park her car on the side street instead of in the usual spot in front of the house.

"And now you're indulging in stealth," she continued as, feeling sneaky, she made her way to the back of the house, hoping to catch Glorimar alone in the kitchen. Not risking the doorbell, she rapped on the glass, and after a few moments Glorimar's anxious face looked out. But anxiety was instantly replaced with relief when Glorimar recognized Nell and bent to unlock the door.

"It's you!" she told Nell. "I'm glad. I've been awfully jumpy lately."

"Are you alone?" Nell looked furtively around the kitchen as if Angela Shilliday might be sitting on a high stool at the counter.

"Yes, quite alone," Glorimar replied. "In fact, alone is what I've mostly been lately. Do you want a cup of tea? I'd love to sit down and have one."

"Perfect," Nell declared. "Just call me Nosey Nellie, Glorimar, but I'm dying to ask what's been going on and I haven't had the nerve or the heart to reach out to Angela."

Glorimar put the kettle on the stove and her expression was grim as spooned loose tea into a pot.

"Missus Shilliday is spending most of the time in her study these days but I don't guess she's working. She sleeps late, then goes up there and sometimes I don't hear a peep from her for hours."

"Where are the children?"

Glorimar sank into the kitchen chair across from Nell and sighed.

"When they got home from the police," she said, "well, not right away but a little time after, Dr. Shilliday took the children away. He took a leave of absence from his practice, and he packed their things—took them right out of school—and took them away to Florida. His mother, Beth, went along too. To help out, I suppose."

Nell frowned. "I thought Angela was to be monitored. Not that she'd be a flight risk," she added hastily, "but I'd understood she wasn't to be alone."

"That's so," Glorimar nodded, "and her sister came out from Michigan to stay with her. But it's funny because they don't spend hardly any time together at all. The sister stays downstairs mostly, reading books in the living room. She's quiet as a mouse. I make them some supper and try to get Missus Shilliday to eat. They sit at the table, those two, but even then they don't say much. And Missus Shilliday looks like she's wasting away."

Glorimar judged the tea had steeped enough and she poured out two cups. Both women gazed silently into their tea as if the future could be read there, in the leaves that had settled in small nests in the depths of the cups. Finally, with a deep sigh of sadness, Glorimar looked up.

"I don't know," she said reflectively. "It's just so sad. That beautiful woman—so smart and all. She'd just bounce through this house, up and down the stairs like a girl Belinda's age. She sure had everything—everything was there for her like it had been set on a silver tray. I can't imagine why she did this— how she got into this mess."

Nell nodded. The fine feeling of the early morning was being replaced by this deep gloom shared with Glorimar. And, in fact, while they had been sitting in the kitchen, gray clouds had overtaken the sun and the air had taken on a faint dampness.

"What do you suppose will happen?" Nell ventured.

Glorimar shrugged. "Just have to wait and see, I guess. Wait and see what the police do. See what the lawyers do. See what Dr. Shilliday does. I figure he's pretty disappointed in his wife."

"He didn't know about the affair with Dr. Povitch, you think?" Nell asked.

"No, I don't think he did," Glorimar answered thoughtfully. "That poor man. On top of all the publicity and shame that his wife's crime has brought the family, he had to hear that she'd been unfaithful too. I think he's gone away to try to heal. And I hope he can. And I think he wanted to get those little girls away from all the hoo-ha that's being kicked up around this whole thing."

"The scandal," Nell supplied.

"Yes," said Glorimar, "that's exactly right. The scandal."

Chapter 33

By Taft University standards, Andrew Povitch's office was commodious. Even so, Nell had to search for a place to sit down, so stuffed was the room with papers, books, manila folders and miscellaneous flotsam and jetsam. Nevertheless Povitch, in greeting her effusively, brayed "Sit down! Sit down!"

Nell looked around, shifted a pile of manila folders off a straight chair and did so. She smiled at the Nobel Prize winner.

"We've met, Dr. Povitch—a couple of times actually—but I doubt if you'll remember."

"And why would you doubt?" he boomed. "I wouldn't forget an attractive woman like you. I recall distinctly that you attended one of my lectures. My great friend Madeline Kaiser introduced us afterwards."

"Yes, and we also met briefly at Angela Shilliday's Christmas party last December."

At this, Povitch frowned slightly.

"That, I don't remember."

The mention of Angela Shilliday seemed to dim his mood

slightly, but perhaps that was just Nell's imagination. The brief cloud across Povitch's face cleared quickly, and he beamed at her as he seated himself across from her at his desk. This seating required him to remove a pile a papers that he placed on the floor.

"Madeline has told me about the ghostwriting plot," he said.

Nell interrupted in protest. "With all due respect, Dr. Povitch, it wasn't a plot. At least it wasn't on my part."

"You should call me Andy," he told her, "and you are right, of course. I'm afraid it was Angela who was keeping the secret."

Povitch suddenly looked very serious.

"Now let me tell you a bit of background of which you may not be aware. Angela Shilliday was a student here at Taft. She left after she'd graduated to do some work in Washington, but when she returned she indicated that she wanted to pursue a doctorate. And so she did, although her progress was a bit sporadic. Stop-start. Stop-start. That was understandable however. She was the young wife of a busy physician and then she became a young mother. Nevertheless, she never completely abandoned the course."

Povitch paused and scratched his jaw in thought. Nell had the impression he was reconstructing a time line.

"Somewhere in there," he said, "the electors on the Nobel Prize committee were thoughtful enough to award the prize in economics to me. To say I was surprised is to understate matters ridiculously. An honor like the Nobel Prize, Nell, causes changes for the honoree that can be cataclysmic. That's what I found anyway. There was a lot of press naturally, but there was also a measure of fame that I felt was richly exaggerated and largely undeserved. But there it is. And it is what it is."

He spread his hands helplessly.

"One day," he continued, "Angela Shilliday came to me with an idea. She proposed that she be allowed to write my biography. My authorized biography. That means, as of course you know, she would proceed with my permission and that permission would ultimately give the book greater authority. Cachet, so to speak. I thought she was mad, but she can be very persistent, and eventually I acquiesced. The process meant that we saw a great deal more of each other than we had formerly done. More, perhaps, than we should have."

Povitch had the grace to look a bit sheepish. Nell did not comment. When he saw she was not going to, he continued.

"At some point, I learned that Angela planned to use the biography as her doctoral thesis, and she wheedled and wangled until she somehow gained permission from her advisors. I suppose her strategy was to realize several benefits from the book. As well as gaining the thesis out of it, she would have her name on the book cover which would buy her a level of fame and veracity. It would boost her standing as well as providing the true story of humble old Andrew Povitch."

Nell waited and was quiet. And Andrew Povitch's voice grew quieter also.

"I did not know—had no idea—that Angela wasn't writing the book herself. I was shocked when Madeline told me that she'd hired a ghostwriter. That she'd hired you. Now, I have nothing at all against ghostwriting. It is an honorable profession. And if Angela had told me that she was collaborating with a professional writer, I would have been fine with that. But I am not fine with her dishonesty nor with her plan to use the work of another for her thesis. The plan to credit herself with original thought and talent she did not possess."

Nell cleared her throat and spoke for the first time.

"Were you paying Angela to write the biography?"

"I was not. The project was her idea, and I believe she intended to eventually sell it to a publisher who would, presumably, take it to the popular market. For Angela, that would mean book tours and book signings as well as possible TV appearances and newspaper interviews and probably a bit of money as well. I don't think she was interested in the money though. There was always plenty of Shilliday money around her. Rather, it was the limelight she craved. The spotlight. Angela likes to have it shining on her."

Nell realized that Povitch had come to the end of his story and was waiting for her to comment.

"Thank you for telling me all this and for giving me the courtesy of your time," she said politely. As he had done earlier, she opened her hands, palm up. "I guess that's that."

Nell moved to rise, but Povitch put out a staying hand.

"Just a minute," he said. "How far did you get with this book?"

"I had completed a solid first draft," Nell told him. "I'd taken Angela's notes and a start she'd made—and a very sketchy start it was, if I may be frank—and I'd done research of my own. That was one of the reasons I asked Madeline to bring me to your lecture—I wanted to see and hear you for myself. Angela had forbidden that."

Povitch shook his head in disgust, but didn't comment.

Nell continued. "We'd had a number of meetings to review the chapters as I wrote them. She'd read them and indicate revisions. Quite a number of revisions sometimes and many with which I didn't agree. But lately—well, from the time of her Christmas party forward—Angela seemed to lose interest in the project. Or perhaps she was just too busy or was distracted, I'm not sure, but our work ground to a halt. But to answer your question, there exists a solid first draft of the manuscript."

"I would like to read it," Andrew Povitch said.

"And I," said Nell, "would be honored if you would."

Chapter 34

"What are you up to now, Nell?"

Robert's pleasant baritone, even over the phone, always lifted Nell's spirits.

"Why-ever do you ask?" she inquired archly.

He chuckled.

"Because I know you and I know you're always up to something. And because I haven't heard from you in a while and that is a strong indication that something is up. And finally, because I am curious. If I stand you to lunch at the Black Cow, can you assuage my curiosity?"

"You don't have to bribe me," Nell told him. "I'd tell you anyway, but I wouldn't say no to a lunch at the Black Cow. Give me the date and time and I'll secure our favorite table under the beadboard arch."

So, good as her word, Nell put her marker down on the favored table and was seated there when she spied Robert's tall form pause at the hostess's stand to inquire. His eyes followed the hostess's directing glance toward Nell, and Robert, ever courteous, took a moment to thank her graciously before making his way across to the dining room to the spot where Nell waited. He bent to kiss her cheek before seating himself across from her in the booth.

"You're looking well," he commented. "That's a good sign."

Nell shrugged.

"I can't think why," she said. "Oh, Robert, I think I'm in the soup again."

Robert arched an eyebrow.

"The last I heard, your client Angela Shilliday was cooling her heels inside Boston Police Headquarters. I assume she was sprung."

"Robert! How you talk! I'm shocked."

But Nell grinned and relented.

"Well, you're right, she was down at police headquarters for a short time. They arrested her and brought her in for questioning. The guy who assaulted Kirsten Wayborne in Downtown Crossing was apparently carrying out the task at the behest of a more sophisticated felon. A hitman. Are you impressed, Robert, by my command of this underworld jargon?"

"Go on," Robert grunted.

"Well the Downtown Crossing guy—his name is Digger Diaz, but I think that's an alias—was very talkative, apparently. The cops claimed he was naming his boss before they even got him to the station. Well, the boss is called Marky Negolian, but there again, Robert, the name means nothing. Evidently everyone on the criminal circuit has a half-dozen names handy."

Robert was patient. He knew Nell well, knew she was a storyteller and a superb one and knew that the whole tale would be told in time.

"The police had entertained Marky Negolian extensively before calling in Angela. He admitted to knowing Digger Diaz—socially, I presume—but wouldn't admit to anything beyond a social acquaintance. He hung Diaz," here Nell eyed Robert archly, "out to dry."

Robert gave her a sour look.

"I don't follow how they made a connection to Angela."

"I was coming to that. The cops didn't give up easily. They kept an eye on Negolian and invited him back a few times, apparently, for more chats. But in the meantime, they were following other avenues to figure out why Kirsten Wayborne was targeted. There didn't seem to be any logical connections between Marky Negolian and a pretty young woman from Taft University."

The waitress arrived, smiled and wondered if Nell and Robert had made up their minds. Robert frowned faintly and uncharacteristically at the interruption, which quietly delighted Nell. She liked a rapt audience.

"I believe I have," she told the waitress graciously. And she ordered the salad that featured apples, dried cranberries and candied walnuts."

"The same," said Robert, and refocused his attention on Nell.

"Where was I?" she asked.

"Connection," Robert supplied. "What was the connection between this Negolian fellow and Kirsten Wayborne?"

"Oh. Yes. I'm getting to that. Well, Kirsten Wayborne had told a detective that she'd received a number of rather threatening emails in the weeks before the assault. The threats were veiled, I believe. Nothing specific. Just warnings to stay away from...ta-*da*! Are you ready for this? Andrew Povitch!"

Robert stared.

"Go on," he said drily. "Tell me how they actually made

that connection."

"Computers. Kirsten Wayborne had deleted the emails and tried to forget about them, but it was easy for the cops to dredge them up. That, along with the Povitch hint, led them back to the source. Angela's office computer at Taft."

Robert gave a low, expressive whistle.

Nell sat back with some satisfaction.

"To continue the tale," she said, "the cops thought they had a pretty good case. They went out to Winchester, arrested Angela and brought her in for questioning, but she was pretty cagey apparently. Didn't admit to anything. Insisted on talking to her lawyer before she gave any details to the police, and in the end, it was determined there were insufficient grounds for charging her. The cops still couldn't figure the Negolian-Waybridge-Angela connection, but at least they had a thread they could pull on. They had to let her go home with Tim Shilliday, but everyone knows she can be re-arrested at any time. And presumably, detectives—and now lawyers probably—are all working to either bring the situation forward or bury it in the dust."

The salads arrived. Nell, parched after her recitation, took a sip of the flinty chardonnay she'd ordered. Sea Glass. She always ordered it at the Black Cow because she liked the name. And, as always, she was mildly disappointed in the taste.

"So two pieces of this thing are linked," said Nell, picking up the pre-salad topic, "Negolian and Diaz. But there is still a puzzle. How do the other pieces fit? Negolian, Waybridge and Angela? How did two women of 'Kirsten's and Angela's backgrounds meet up with a thug like Negolian?"

But Robert, with a shake of his head, had no answers.

"I seem to recall you saying at the start of this story, that you are in the soup again." Robert addressed his salad.

"Umm. That's another long story."

"It was a long drive up here," Robert told her. "You might as well make it worthwhile."

"Well, I was in the house, working with Angela, when the police came to arrest her. I'd told you that, hadn't I?"

Robert nodded.

"That session was the last work we did together on Andrew Povitch's biography. I stopped in once to see Glorimar and sort of take the temperature of the house and family. At that point, Tim Shilliday had taken his mother and the little girls and gone off to Florida to lick wounds, to recover, to do I don't know what. Angela was at home, pretty much confined to the house, and her sister had come from somewhere in Michigan to stay with her. Keep her company, I suppose, and keep an eye on her. According to Glorimar, the place was like a mausoleum. Angela was hardly speaking, even to her sister. It was all very sad. I'm sure she didn't feel like working on the book, and I certainly wasn't going to open the subject with her."

"Have you seen her since that day?"

"Since she was arrested? No. And I haven't called either, and I think I'm beginning to feel a little bit bad about that."

Nell dug into her salad in search of another one of those candied walnuts. They were delicious.

"But that's not all," she told Robert, not looking up.

He watched her mining process and waited. Robert Hutchins was a patient man.

"While all of Taft apparently, is buzzing with gossip—first about the assault and then about the arrest—my new friend Madeline Kaiser got together with Andrew Povitch. You remember Madeline, of course."

"Certainly."

"Well, you see Robert, they are old friends from way back. Way back in Ohio. And as they were talking, she told him that

Angela had hired a ghost to write the biography. Namely, me. Do you remember that song from *Lil Abner*. Robert, *Namely Me*?"

Robert shook his head. "Just continue please."

"Well, I guess he was shocked. Then a little angry. Then curious. He asked to meet me. So we met and we talked and he wanted to know all about the biography. Said he hadn't cared much about the idea when Angela first proposed it, but he'd gotten curious and he was getting to like the idea of having an authorized biography. So he asked me questions about ghostwriting—you know the usual questions people always ask—and he asked me how I charged. Again, the usual questions. Then he said he wanted to see the draft."

Nell sat back, giving every indication that her narration was finished. Robert wasn't satisfied though.

"And what did you say? What did you do?"

"I gave him the draft."

"That's it?"

"Well, it is for now. He's reading it presumably. I have no idea what's going to happen. But Robert, what if he wants to hire me? 'A man cannot serve two masters'."

The check arrived, disguised modestly within a vinyl folder. Robert swiped it toward himself and examined the evidence. Eschewing the ballpoint provided by the Black Cow, he selected his own fountain pen from an inside pocket, added in the tip and signed his name. Robert C. Hutchins. Very distinguished.

"Wait and see what happens," he said.

Chapter 35

Andrew Povitch slapped the manuscript down on the table.

"It has no soul," he said.

Nell's face bloomed into radiance.

"I know!" she said joyously.

Povitch regarded her curiously.

"You know? And you're happy about that?"

Nell nodded enthusiastically. "I'd been telling Angela exactly that, but she kept on bleeding it—bleeding it white. Taking things out, adding stilted phrases back in, and refusing to let me go where I wanted to go, which was—for one thing—to you. I needed personal interviews. Contact. Touch! As you say, soul."

Andrew Povitch was staring at her, but he slowly began to nod. Then he began to grin.

"If you can put soul into this, Nell Bane, I think we'll have ourselves a living, breathing biography of that wretched old sinner Andy Povitch. An *authorized* biography. When Angela proposed the idea of a biography, my reaction was rather tepid.

Who would want to read a biography of *me*? But now that I've read this and can see what might be possible, I rather like the idea. Yes, I like it very much indeed. And I'd like you to continue the project. Of course you'll have to go back and add soul... can you do that Nell Bane?"

Nell had been nodding her vigorous excitement and confidence, but her blissful expression was slowly fading. She could see a problem.

"What about Angela Shilliday?"

"What about her?"

"She was...is...my client. She was the one who hired me to write this book."

"And are you still working for her?" Povitch demanded.

Nell was confused, She tried to sort this out.

"I guess I'm probably not," she said slowly. "We haven't worked on this for what feels like ages. The ball was in her court when the work stalled and she's never batted it back."

"Do you think she's going to?" Povitch asked gently.

"Honestly?" Nell said, "No. She's got her hands full. Her passion for the project must be drained out and even if she's not convicted of being an accessory to attempted murder, I can't see how she'd ever want to resurrect this project."

"Did you have a contract with Angela?"

"Not a written one," Nell replied. "Nothing formal. But we did have a firm understanding. The terms were one third of the quoted price to start the writing process, and she has paid that. The second third was due when the complete first draft was achieved—which, by the way, would have been now—and the final third was to be paid upon completion."

"Did you receive the second payment?"

"No."

"Well, there you are then."

Andrew Povitch made a gesture suggesting that the whole

case had been wrapped up neatly and presented to Nell.

"You fulfilled the first part of your contract, for which you were paid. Case closed. You actually fulfilled the second third, although it wasn't delivered nor paid for. The contract, however—such as it was—is nullified. Therefore," he summarized, "there is no problem. Shall we begin? Tell me what you would charge to write my story."

Nell did.

"Now you must tell me all manner of things," Nell said to him, placing the Sony recorder on the table. "Tell me about Cleveland, tell me about Ohio State, tell me what it was like to visit Europe and see Slovenia for the first time. Tell me what it's like to be Andrew Povitch. Tell me your stories."

Chapter 36

And now Nell was beginning to write—to write with the freedom that had been denied her—to write unfettered, challenged to make Andrew Povitch come alive on the pages. She opened a new file on the computer—a clean file—and started afresh. Soul, that's what she needed to pour into Andrew Povitch's biography. She closed her eyes and let the writing part of her mind look inward, waited to hear the music and the sound of distant conversations between people she did not yet know. All she had to do was listen. Listen, and then write.

#

He was asleep when the call came—what is known as the Magic Call. The alarm clock hadn't yet announced the day's beginning, and at first he thought the ringing phone was part of the dream. Still, when the insistent phone rang on, Andrew Povitch stirred himself enough to grope for the receiver. The caller spoke perfect English, but there was just a trace of something foreign, more of a cadence than an accent.

"Dr. Andrew Povitch?"

Povitch had to clear his throat twice before successfully acknowledging this.

"I am Soren Gustafson. I am given the pleasant task of informing you that you have won the Sveriges Riksbank Prize in Economic Sciences in Memory of Alfred Nobel."

"I thought it was a dream," Povitch marveled later. "I'd been dreaming of a wide lawn where people were playing some kind of lawn game—croquet perhaps or bocce. And then a dinner bell rang—I think it was a dinner bell—and a group of people swept by, the way people do in dreams, and they were all going somewhere. I grabbed the phone by force of habit even though I knew I was meant to go with the crowed of people, and what Dr. Gustafson said made no sense to me whatsoever. No sense at all."

Remembering this, Andrew Povitch laughs. His laugh is huge. Wide. Born from somewhere deep below his lungs. He continues his tale.

"I told him he was joking," Povitch remembers. "'You're joking!' I said.

Gustafson had laughed. He was enjoying himself.

"No. No joke, he said, and he talked on, explaining. Congratulating. Povitch mentally stumbling along,

"I had no idea at the time what he was saying," Povitch said later. "I knew all the words he used—I could have told you what each one meant—but when the words were strung together, there was no meaning. My brain had forgotten how to function. How to interpret."

But it didn't matter. In the end, it would all be clear. Everything would happen just as it should, like the tumblers of a complicated lock clicking and snapping into place. There would be the announcement splashed across front pages of newspapers and told excitedly on the TV news. In Boston, the media commotion would be especially big since now the city had another Nobel winner; not the first certainly, but in places such as Boston, these things are counted over and inventoried—valued like bits of whelk on a woven strap of wampum. There would be the obligatory trip to Stockholm for the awards ceremony (and for more publicity) and the cash prize itself. There would be interviews and appearances. Taft University, borrowing some of Povitch's glory, would twirl into the spotlight, because a Nobel winner on the faculty was good for the institution's prestige quotient. And for business.

At the conclusion of Soren Gustafson's call, Andrew Povitch hung up the phone quietly. He was sitting now in his underwear on the edge of the bed, trying to make sense of what had just happened. The dream of the people on the lawn hadn't quite evaporated. People still milled confusedly in his brain. For the rest of his days, Povitch would associate the Nobel Prize for Economics with a wide green lawn on a summer day and the sound of croquet balls or bocce balls tunking and the noise of a ringing bell.

He reached for the phone again. From memory he tapped in the number of Madeline Kaiser, friend and colleague since student days at Ohio State.

"Maddie, the strangest thing has just happened. The most extraordinary thing!"

Madeline Kaiser was an early riser and at 5:45 was already making coffee in her kitchen. More quickly than Povitch had, she grasped the message and translated what it meant. What it would mean. Her scream of astonishment and excitement brought Povitch into reality.

"I'm on my way to the office," he shouted, galvanized. "Meet me there in thirty minutes!"

#

Back in Cleveland, no one would have predicted Andrew Povitch would one day be a Nobel laureate. He was simply Frank and Anna's boy, one of the rowdier kids on his block of East 143rd Street. A good kid, a likeable boy, and if he happened to pound a baseball through your living room window, you could be sure Andy Povitch would own up to it. He'd be right up on your front porch, offering to have the window repaired even if he had to work off the cost by lawn mowing or snow shoveling.

But that's the way things were in the Slovenian neighborhood of Collinwood where people were decent and hardworking. Not fancy like folks up in the Heights, but people who held strong values. People who were respectful of others and were steeped in well-earned self respect.

Frank and Anna Povitch left Slovenia as Displaced Persons—DPs—right after the Second World War. But they had relatives in Cleveland, and they knew they would be welcomed. DPs they might have been, but Frank and Anna were invested with dignity, willingly worked hard and saved their money. Frank found a good job at the Fisher Body auto assembly plant and Anna took on employment in a bakery on St. Clair. They saved enough to buy the top half of a two-story house—a nice house with a deep front porch from which small Andy could see up and down the street from St. Clair on the south and, looking north, could image the blue of Lake Erie just out of view.

"That was a great place to grow up!" he declares.

Not everyone would have thought so.

The street, running north and south, was solidly built out with close-set neighboring houses that blocked much of each other's light. Behind the tree lawns, front yards were no wider than the houses they aproned, too small, most of them to support gardens or landscape plantings. Still, many neighbors planted their backyards with pocket-sized vegetable plots and small grape arbors.

The autumn air was perfumed with the scent of grapes and Andy, walking home from school, sniffed the promise of coming harvest and a dinner table laid with a clean cotton cloth and delicious Slovenian food. For Anna Povitch was a star cook. At St. Mary's Sodality and the local Slovenian National Home, everyone said so. Her nut-filled *potica* was exceptional and was probably the reason the bakery was careful to keep Anna on staff. Frank's lunch pail and the brown bag Andrew carried to school were stuffed with the sort of food Anna regarded as proper. Not for her men were there Wonder Bread sandwiches made of baloney or peanut butter. Meat and potatoes for Frank. For little Andrew too, until he complained his lunches weren't like those of the other kids. Anna disapproved, but she made American sandwiches for her boy. It was important that he fit in.

Povitch fit in like a size seven hand fits a size seven glove. He was popular at school, and when he left St. Mary's after the eighth grade to go to Collinwood High School, he rapidly became a standout student and a credible athlete.

"I was no star quarterback," Povitch admits, "but I liked everything about football. The sound of helmet hitting helmet. The way your cleats dug into the sod. The night games under the lights when the fall air was sharp. In those days people raked their leaves into the streets and banked them along the curbs. Then after dark, they dropped lighted matches, and the nights smelled of burning leaves. You rarely smell that now. But even so, when I do catch a whiff of leaves burning, the scent takes me right back to Cleveland and those night games at Collinwood and walking home afterward with the girl-of-the-moment—with Karen Kapel or Bev Jeanes."

Povitch keeps a prom photograph in his office. Almost unrecognizable as a skinny kid with a flattop haircut and a white dinner jacket, his date is Mira Hanzak, his future wife. Tall and blonde, she is wearing a ballerina-length gown of layered net and her high-heeled slippers are clear plastic, designed to show off a pretty, naked foot. In the photo, she looks more mature than her husband-to-be who is grinning with delight to be there on this grown-up night with this lovely girl. But there are no signs that the eager-looking young man is a future Nobel laureate.

# # #

The International Conference on Applied Business and Economics was held in Geneva, Switzerland that year, and Dr. Andrew Povitch was listed as a presenter. The point of ICABE was to present an open forum—a place for academics and professionals from a number of varied fields to meet and exchange ideas. For people interested in business and economics, the ICABE was a mecca and an opportunity to meet people inside and outside their own disciples. For Andrew Povitch, the ICABE was his first foot onto the international stage.

Povitch was astonished when the audience burst into whole-hearted applause at the conclusion of his paper. He looked up from the podium in wonder, looked out over the smiling, clapping herd of economists and business people. Although most presenters left the stage to the accompaniment of some applause, it was rarely more than a polite pattering and occasionally—and embarrassingly—the applause was the effort of a mere half a dozen or so determined souls— colleagues of the presenter, no doubt—stoutly coming to the support of one of their own. But the reception for Povitch's work was lengthy and spontaneously enthusiastic. And at the reception afterward, his hand was pumped time and again and his shoulder was good-heartedly thumped to the point of pain by people congratulating and complimenting him.

Ecological economics, the field that Povitch had chosen to pioneer, was quite new and in the awakening of this "green" consciousness, his work was exciting. Moreover, he was able to clearly draw the distinctions between his discipline and the field of environmental economics with which it was often confused. Povitch had the gift for clarity, for precision, for bringing the nuts and bolts of a new subject to an uninformed audience without talking down to them or without over-complicating the topic. Moreover, he had an easy affect and knew how to infuse his technical presentation with flashes of humor. His was a rare gift, and the conference-goers were appreciative and impressed.

Andrew Povitch was on the way to making a name for himself.

Chapter 37

Once more Nell stood looking up at the house built in 1924, not in 1925. Preparing to ring the bell, she thought of the first time she'd stood there and flashed on all that had happened to the family inside this house since she first met Angela Shilliday. From Glorimar, she'd learned that Tim Shilliday had returned home with the little girls and that Angela's sister had gone back to Michigan.

"Is she seeing anybody? Angela, I mean," Nell had asked. "Do you think she'd see me?"

"It's been like a funeral home around here," Glorimar said candidly. "Nobody comes or goes except Beth sometimes. Him and her don't talk hardly at all. Even the girls are quiet. They're back in school though, and that's good for them."

Nell suddenly imagined a dollhouse. The handsome house in Winchester flashed up with one entire wall cut away so she could see all the floors at once with the elegant window treatments and the furniture all in place. She wondered who was billeted in the snoratorium.

149

But after delivering her current events report, Glorimar came around to answering Nell's question.

"Would she see you? I honestly don't know. I guess you'd have to ask her."

And so Nell had.

The phone conversation had been odd. Subdued.

"I've been thinking a lot about you, Angela, and I've been concerned—well, naturally one would be."

(Oh dear! That sounded terrible.)

Nell blundered on.

"Well I was wondering—that is, I *wondered*—if I could stop in for a visit. Just a short one. Not to work or anything, just for a social visit, friend-to-friend."

Nell offered this last statement awkwardly. She and Angela had never been friends. Employer-employee. Client-supplier. Older woman-younger woman. Did any of those descriptors fit?

There was silence on the other end of the line, and Nell was preparing to apologize, ring off, and dismiss the entire attempt as a well-intentioned impulse rebuffed, when to her surprise, Angela answered.

"Okay. I guess that'd be alright." She paused.

Nell had the impression she was considering.

"I've shut myself away like some hermit. I guess I could do with some company."

And now, as Nell prepared to ring the bell, she felt a flutter of something like stage fright. Glorimar answered the bell promptly as if she'd been standing right behind the door. She and Nell greeted each other with a formality that disguised the closeness they had come to share in the last weeks.

"Is she up in her study?" Nell asked softly.

Glorimar shook her head.

"She's in there. In the den."

Nell knew the way, although she'd never sat in the den. It was off the hall that narrowed from the wide foyer. Nell stuck her head around the door into the room. Angela Shilliday was sitting in the exact center of a sofa. Her eyes were unfocused; she was looking at absolutely nothing at all.

"Knock-knock," said Nell gently.

Angela's head swiveled to look at her.

"Hello. Come in."

She did not move. So Nell tramped into the room and sat in a club chair directly opposite Angela Shilliday. Once seated, she couldn't think of a single sensible thing to say. Not the weather, not Angela's appearance—which wasn't exactly blooming—not even the work that had brought them together.

Nell brought both hands down on both her knees with a slap that was louder than she'd intended.

"Well! Here we are."

Angela looked at her as if she were mad.

"Well, obviously, we're here... oh hell, look Angela," Nell blurted. "We had—maybe we still have, I don't know—a business relationship, and I would like to know where, in your opinion, that relationship stands."

Angela took her time answering. To Nell, she appeared to be trying to think. Her affect was flat—flat as cheap paint on a sheetrock wall. There was no depth. No spark. Nothing seemed to be going on inside. Nell waited.

Angela spread her hands. Her fingers, Nell noted, were long and pretty even with the nails now plain and unvarnished.

"I don't know. I can't think," she said simply. "Everything is just . . . just nothing. Waiting . . . yes, that's it—the waiting. I can't do anything, can't focus on anything until I know what . . . well . . . until what's going to happen. And until it happens."

Nell nodded. She understood this, and her voice was gentle.

"Angela. Do you think you will ever again pick up the threads of writing Andrew Povitch's biography?"

Angela Shilliday looked as if she were swallowing an egg. A very large egg. Her eyes were wide and her long, lovely throat was making swallowing motions. Then her chin began to quiver and she shook her head.

"I can't . . . " She shook her head until her hair swished from side to side. "I could never..."

But Nell came out of her chair in one swift, fluid movement, knelt on the floor and covered Angela's hands with both of her own.

"It's okay," she said soothingly. "It's okay. You don't have to do anything. You don't have to make any decisions. Nothing. Your job now is to do your best to put all this behind you. To take whatever comes and be strong with it. Strong for your family, for your children and your husband. Strong for yourself."

Nell punctuated this little speech with a hard squeeze on Angela's hand and a confident nod of her head. Angela's eyes were still wide and bright with tears that she wouldn't allow to brim over but her chin was no longer quivering.

Nell rocked back on her heels, then pulled her fanny up into the club chair. She struck her knees again. "I wish I'd stop doing that!" a part of her mind scolded.

"Well, here's the thing," she began. "Dr. Povitch wants his biography. Apparently he's become enamored with the idea, and he asked a friend of his to get in touch with me and see if I'd continue working on it. Not as a ghostwriter—as myself. As Nell Bane. And I wouldn't feel comfortable doing that without speaking to you and getting your permission."

Angela Shilliday looked stunned. Nell wondered if she was thinking that this was just one more piece of evil luck to be aimed at her head. On the other hand, Angela didn't look like she was thinking. She simply looked confused. And hurt. For a moment Nell saw the chin quiver again. Then Angela Shilliday pulled herself together. She sat up straighter and she looked Nell directly in the eye. Now Nell saw once more the Angela Shilliday who was familiar.

She started to speak. "I! I! ..."

Then she seemed to deflate. The air just seemed to leave her and she slumped back into the sofa and shook her head. She waved her hand back and forth in a shooing motion.

"I don't care," she said. "Do what you want. Andrew isn't ... well it doesn't matter anymore. Andrew doesn't ... can't .. . matter anymore."

Nell couldn't think of anything more to say. So the two women sat in silence for some time. Nell had no idea how long they sat like that. If she'd had to ascribe a color to the silence, Nell would have chosen gray. No, maybe brown. But some color that was sad; something hopeless. And she felt as miserable as Angela must.

Finally Nell cleared her throat.

"I'll just be going," she explained. "I can see myself out."

She said this quickly as though Angela had made a hostess-sort of move to walk her to the door. But Angela hadn't moved. Nell paused.

"Well. Let me wish you all the ...

The what? The best? All success? Luck?

"Let me wish you the strength you will need to get through this difficult time," she said. "Strength, yes, to see you safely to the other side of it. And then peace. I will wish for you peace."

But in the hall, Nell turned left toward the kitchen instead of the other way toward the front door. Glorimar was writing a grocery list. She looked up but she didn't smile.

Nell shook her head.

"I was no help at all," she confessed. "Oh Glorimar, I'm

afraid this visit was just for me. Just to ease my guilty conscience and I was no help to Angela at all."

Glorimar sighed.

"There's just so much you can do," she said quietly. "Just so much any of us can do. Missus Shilliday made this bed, and now it's hers to lie in."

Chapter 38

"You never ask me about glazes," Bunty Whitney said peevishly. "Or grades of clay. No, all you're interested in is psych stuff— why so-and-so is a jerk or why such-and-such is narcissistic."

Nell looked humbly contrite. Or hoped she did anyway.

Bunty relented.

"Okay. What is it this time?"

"I went to see Angela Shilliday," Nell told her. "I needed to tell her about Povitch asking me to work on his biography."

"Meaning you needed to confess," Bunty said perceptively, "and you were seeking absolution."

Nell didn't know whether to be relieved or annoyed by her neighbor's perspicacity.

"Well," Bunty relented, "what did she say? Did she give you her blessing?"

"Not in so many words," Nell said carefully. "At first she was like a zombie. Sort of numb-acting, like nothing held any interest for her."

Bunty nodded.

"That's reasonable. She's had a tremendous upheaval in her life, and she has plunged from the pinnacle of having everything to the pit of having nothing. She's teetering on the verge of being arrested for her suspected part in a contract murder. Her husband has discovered she was cuckolding him, so he feels betrayed, and furthermore, her notoriety must be excruciatingly embarrassing for a man in his position—a physician with patients and a reputation to maintain. In fact, the entire Shilliday family must feel humiliated. She doesn't know what's going to happen to her—whether or not her husband will stay married to her and what will happen to her children if he doesn't. She's got to be wondering whether there will be a trial, and if there is a trial, whether there will be a conviction and a horrible sentence. And even if legal things work out okay, can the damage that's been done be repaired? And finally, she no longer has Andrew Povitch. And she knows it. Isn't that enough to turn anyone into a zombie?"

Nell was nodding.

"All of that is true."

"Well," said Bunty. "Did you ask permission to work with Andrew Povitch? Or did you simply tell her that is what you intend to do?"

"I didn't exactly do either. I just said that he'd approached me."

"And she ... what?" prompted Bunty.

"For just a second, there was a flash of anger," Nell said carefully, remembering. "For just an instant, I could see the old Angela. Then she slipped back into that shroud of misery. In the end, I don't think she really cared."

"So do you infer permission?"

"Yes," Nell said slowly, "I guess I'm cleared for take-off. I guess I need to shuck off any guilt feelings and go ahead. I'm seeing Povitch next week, as a matter of fact. I have a draft to show him. I need to prove to him that I can write with soul."

"Now," said Bunty decisively, "how about making some of that half-assed taco soup of yours."

"I beg your pardon. What are you talking about?"

"That stuff that's supposed to taste Mexican," Bunty elucidated, "except it's not. It's good though."

Nell thought.

"Oh, you mean that soup that cheats with the taco seasoning and the ranch dressing packet?"

"Bingo!" Bunty declared. "The very one!"

HALF-ASSED TACO SOUP

1 pound of ground turkey
1 large onion, coarsely chopped
1 clove of garlic, chopped
1 envelope of taco seasoning
1 envelope of ranch dressing mix
1 19-oz. can of red kidney beans
1 19-oz. can of cannelloni beans
1 19-oz. can of chickpeas
2 14-oz cans of fire-roasted tomatoes
1 can of corn
1 small can of chopped chilies (optional)
4 cups of chicken broth

So to repay Bunty for her patience and wisdom, and to atone for failing to ask about Bunty's passionate interest in glazes and grades of clay, Nell began browning the turkey in a large pot, then added the onion and garlic to sweat. When she'd judged the meat to be adequately browned, she stirred in the contents of the taco and ranch packets. Then she added the broth, the tomatoes, the beans and corn. She searched the pantry for a can of chilies but since the search proved futile, she omitted the chilies from the recipe. After the soup came to a boil, Nell turned the heat low, covered the pot and left the soup to simmer and steep. And when she finally served it up, Bunty happily crumbled some crisp taco shells over the surface of the soup and sprinkled on some grated cheddar cheese.

Ole!

Chapter 39

Tish Penney, once she got her teeth into a good story, refused to let it go. She hung on like a bulldog grips a woodchuck, and she finally caught a break when Marky Negolian—in a command performance at police headquarters—tried to cut a plea deal.

New Revelations in Wayborne Assault Case
by Tish Penney

Hitman Marky Negolian, long under suspicion by police for his possible connection to the assault in an MBTA station on Taft University co-ed Kirsten Wayborne, attempted to cut a plea deal yesterday by finally confessing to his part in a murder plot.

According to Negolian, he was hired by Angela Shilliday of Winchester to push Kirsten Wayborne of Newton into the path of an on-coming MBTA train. Negolian claims that Shilliday offered him the sum of $5,000 to carryout out the assault.

"She sent mixed messages," Negolian stated. "I was confused. She

didn't want a violent murder. But non-violent murder—isn't that what they call a contradiction of terms?"

Shilliday and Wayborne were acquainted through their associations with Taft University where both are affiliated with the Economics Department. Shilliday is a candidate in the doctoral program and a part-time instructor; Wayborne is a student in the graduate program. The assault plot followed a series of threatening emails that Shilliday allegedly sent to Wayborne warning her to stay away from Dr. Andrew Povitch. Povitch, a winner of the Nobel Prize in Economics, is a professor at Taft and was allegedly carrying on an affair with Shilliday, although it appears that the relationship was waning. Shilliday apparently suspected Povitch of starting up an intimate relationship with Ms. Wayborne.

According to Negolian, Shilliday told him that Wayborne was "a threat to a personal relationship" and she wanted that threat removed. She did not specifically name Povitch, although she did specify that she wanted the "removal" to be conducted through non-violent means.

"I had a hard time figuring that one out," Negolian is quoted as saying. "I mean how do you rub out someone out gently? In the end we settled on the train idea because it wasn't like pulling a knife or shooting a gun. It was an arms-length attack, so to speak."

Shilliday allegedly paid Negolian $2,500 to instigate the plot with the remainder to be paid upon a satisfactory outcome. Negolian subcontracted the assault to Digger Diaz, a petty thug well known to police for small crimes.

"Diaz can't pick his nose correctly," Negolian said during the arraignment. "He gives her a shove and runs like hell, then whines to me when I won't hand over the money."

Angela Shilliday was arrested briefly shortly after the assault, but was released because there were insufficient grounds for holding her. Her re-arrest and arraignment is expected soon.

Nell Bane, reading the story, shook her head sadly. One less thing for Angela Shilliday to wonder about.

Chapter 40

"So Nell Bane," Andrew Povitch's voice boomed out of the phone receiver, "you've certainly shown you can write with soul! I definitely wish to engage you to write my biography. Please consider this a formal commitment until I next see you and we can establish a written contract. Now. What are we calling this opus?"

"I thought we could title it *The Economics of a Life: Andrew Povitch*. How does that sound?"

"*The Economics of a Life*," he repeated slowly. "Let me consider that for a while, but … yes. Yes. I think I like it very much."

"It didn't take you long to consider," Nell observed. "Do you always make up your mind that quickly?"

"I am decisive, yes," he stated. "The way to get something done is to go right at it hammer and tongs."

"*Hammer and Tongs*," said Nell thoughtfully. "*The Life Story of a Nobel Laureate*. That would work too."

"I think you'll bring a fresh muse to this project, Nell

Bane," Povitch told her. "We'll be a good team. How do we best go about it?"

"We'll meet regularly," Nell told him. "We'll review what I've written and you will tell me more stories which I will go away and write about. Name the date and time for us to formally begin."

Povitch did.

Nell was gratified. She was going to enjoy getting into the work of writing Povitch's biography without the weight of Angela Shilliday leaning over her shoulder, editorializing and nit-picking everything from vocabulary to semicolons. She'd look forward to meeting with Povitch in his office at Taft.

On the arranged date, they worked solidly and companionably for more than an hour on the drafts she had supplied, but at the end of the session, Povitch pushed back from his desk and tipped back in his chair. He sighed a sigh that came from somewhere deep in mind and gut.

"Troubling stuff," he said.

Nell looked up sharply. Was he starting to criticize her work now?

But seeing her worried look, Povitch hurried to set matters straight.

"No, no, not you. It's all this stuff with Angela. I feel terrible about it. About everything. And I can't help feeling responsible."

"Not for everything surely," Nell said, realizing as she spoke that she was damning him slightly by her choice of words. "You certainly didn't push Kirsten Wayborne in front of the train nor send her threatening emails."

She shook her head.

"I really don't understand it," she said. "I got to know Angela during the months we worked together, and I can't believe she is capable of such things. She is a very focused person, I always knew that. When she has a goal, she moves toward it with unwavering passion but I didn't think she could mow down anything that got in her way. She is used to getting what she wants, but I can't reconcile that with her wish to harm an innocent person."

"Perhaps to Angela, Kirsten wasn't innocent," Povitch offered. "And I'm certainly not innocent. Perhaps it was a way to get at me. To harm me."

Nell was beginning to feel like Bunty Whitney, backed into the position of supplying the psychological reasons for the actions of another—a role for which she was truly unqualified. She felt like she was treading in very deep waters.

"Maybe that's why Angela focused on Kirsten Wayborne— because she was vulnerable. Angela knew she wouldn't fight back because she was unaware of what was going on. Kirsten didn't even know she had an enemy."

The pair sat in silence. The atmosphere in Povitch's cluttered office, as well as the light outside, had darkened.

"It looks like this unfortunate matter is headed for the courts," Povitch offered glumly.

"Oh dear," Nell murmured. Then she had a thought. "Will you have to testify, do you think? Might you be called into this mess?"

He shrugged.

"Might," he said. "I don't know. I've heard nothing so far, but lawyers move with the speed of glaciers sometimes."

He seemed lost in thought.

"I *am* guilty though."

Nell started to protest again, but he waved her words away.

"Women!" he said it as an oath, "They are my nemesis. Always women! But look, Nell. We've had a good session and I don't wish to end on a sour note."

He waved his arm over the papers on the desk.

"Do you have enough work here to keep you busy for a week or so?"

"Absolutely."

Nell began gathering and stacking the indicated sheets of manuscript. Then she looked up quickly.

"Don't think too much about this situation," she advised. "It will be what it's going to be, and I am confident that it will all even out in the end."

She smiled and Povitch returned her smile.

But once outside his office, Nell paused and frowned in thought. Then, instead of turning right toward the stairs, she turned left. Madeline Kaiser had said she had the roomnext door to Povitch. Cautiously Nell put her head around the doorjamb of the adjoining office.

"Are you at home to company?"

Madeiline Kaiser looked up and smiled.

"Andrew thinks he may be called to testify if there's a trial," Nell said, coming into the office.

Madeline nodded.

"He's not the only one. I've just been told I will be subpoenaed as a character witness for Kirsten. For the prosecution."

Nell's eyebrows went up.

"To quote Bette Davis," Madeline Kaiser said, "Fasten your seatbelts. It's going to be a bumpy ride."

Chapter 41

Angela's arrest came quietly—undetected even by the voracious Tish Penney. With her husband at her side, Angela appeared once again at Boston Police Headquarters and submitted to the arrest proceedings. She carried a small overnight bag, spent the night in jail as a guest of the city, and in the morning rejoined her husband in a sleepy courtroom for the arraignment and bail posting. Angela's lawyer, George "The Grinder" Grenier, walked resolutely beside the Shillidays, shielding them with his wide shoulders and slicing through procedure and red tape with the professional practice born of long experience. By ten in the morning, Tim Shilliday's black BMW was slipping out of the city. Glorimar, waiting at the house in Winchester, reported all this to Nell later in a phone call.

Nell felt depressed. A trial was coming alright. Helpless, she brooded for a while, cleaned the refrigerator, wandered into the little-used front rooms and dusted. But in the end she could think of nothing else to do but make soup. She paged despondently through her collection of soup recipes, discarded several because she didn't have the on hand and in the end, chose escarole soup.

ESCAROLE SOUP

I large onion, peeled and coarsely chopped
1 T minced garlic
Canola oil as needed
Kosher salt
4 c chicken stock
1 pound sweet Italian sausage, cut in coins and browned in the oven at 350
1/2 pound of escarole, cut in ribbons, then in 2" pieces
1 can fire-roasted tomatoes
1 T fish sauce
2 t lemon juice or white vinegar
cayenne pepper (optional)

Sweat the onion in soup pot with oil. Season with a three-finger pinch of kosher salt, add stock and bring to a simmer. Add sausage, greens, tomato, fish sauce and lemon juice and cook just till greens are wilted. Taste and adjust the seasonings with fish sauce or lemon juice.

Chapter 42

Nell polished up the draft and shipped it off to Andrew Povitch. He would read it one final time and pass it along to his publisher. There would still be work to do when the galleys came back, Nell knew that. But just twitches and hitches, a nip here, a tuck there would be required, and that would be pleasant enough; Nell liked polishing.

Because she had been working hard for a long time on the Povitch biography, her housework had deteriorated and the antique cottage on the Newburyport backstreet, also needed polishing. And it needed attention immediately. So in the waning days of the dark winter, Nell got busy washing woodwork and polishing windows gone dull with winter salt from the road and spray from the sea.

In her studio, Bunty Whitney had a big project going. A shop in town had given her a huge order for mugs, and Bunty was throwing clay and pulling handles at all hours. Nell, who kept an eye on Bunty's studio across the back lot, saw the lights burning late. She made a mental note to pry Bunty out of there as soon as possible and spirit her off for a long lunch or a short road trip.

But when she suggested it, Bunty complained.

"Just because you have a break in your work," she said, "doesn't mean I can kick mine aside and run off baying at the moon with you."

Nell started to be contrite, but Bunty wiped her clay-caked fingers on her smock.

"What did you have in mind?"

"An antique crawl?" Nell suggested. "We could take a day and meander down Route 1A, then down 133 and make a pact to stop into every single antique shop we see along the way."

"Well, then," said Bunty heartily. "I don't need to throw mugs every single moment of my life. How about tomorrow if the weather's fine?"

But the weather wasn't fine the next day. Nor the day after that. A nor'easter blew in, smashing rain all over Nell's newly-washed windows and dampening her spirits. And the antique crawl had to be put off.

The nor'easter blew itself out. Eventually. It took ten days, however, for temperatures to recover and allow spring to present its teasing face and to tempt Nell's thoughts toward e.e. cummings.

"He is the quintessential springtime poet," she told Bunty, who replied "Uh."

"*O sweet, spontaneous earth,*" quoted Nell exaltedly lowering her car window and inhaling deeply. "And then this: ...*thou answerest them only ... with ... spring.*"

Bunty stared.

Nell didn't care. She quoted on: "*In justspring ... when the world is ... puddlewonderful...* Don't you just love that, Bunty? Puddlewonderful."

"Nell," Bunty said pragmatically. "Dear. Get a grip. Think

potholes. Think pollen and sinuses. Think bee stings and crabgrass. Think court date."

For Bunty was correct. Angela Shilliday's trial date was scheduled at The Suffolk Superior Court for Criminal Justice in Boston, and Nell knew she'd be drawn there as surely as a bee in springtime is drawn to a blossom.

But today, driving down Route 133 and into Essex, there could indeed be cautious optimism that winter had finally slunk off, even though Nell and Bunty both knew that the weather could still turn around and bite them with a spring snowstorm. Cautious New Englanders were careful to remind each other of that freak snowstorm in May of '77 that snapped all the magnolia branches when they were in full flower.

"Imagine! Shoveling all that snow in May!" Bunty, remembering, was indignant all over again. "All that damage! I remember that Worcester got over a foot."

Nell sympathized.

"I simply couldn't face it," she said. "Look, Bunty—The Elephant's Trunk! We have to dive in there!"

And she clicked on her turn signal and drove Bunty right up to the Elephant's door.

At the end of the day Nell had a nice addition to her collection of blue and white Spode plates as well as a fragment of a cement pediment that she planned to station in the garden, and Bunty—unaccountably—had purchased a graduated set of vernier calipers. Moreover, she had been seduced by an old wooden sign that read FISH. They'd had quite a time forcing it into the backseat of Nell's Saab.

"What the hell was I thinking?" Bunty asked Nell when the two women finally climbed out of the car in Newburyport and had wrenched FISH out as well.

But Nell had no answer.

"Oh well," Bunty said cheerfully, "It'll be a good talking

point."

"How about coming in for a cup of tea," Nell suggested.

"How about coming in for a glass of wine?" Bunty bargained wickedly.

"Done."

Nell was grateful for the day's respite, for she knew the pleasant winds were about to shift and she would be making her way into Boston on a daily basis to be present for Angela Shilliday's trial.

Chapter 43

It didn't take Tish Penney long to discover that Angela Shilliday had been re-arrested—this time on the charge of solicitation to commit first degree murder. The journalist snooped, questioned, dug, wheedled, bullied and tried everything short of bribery to learn how the police had gained enough evidence to arrest her again. The case cracked because Mark Negolian finally cracked.

Marky Negolian Holds Key to Shilliday
Conspiracy Case
By Tish Penney

Police detectives have been aware for some time that known felon Marky Negolian was the key to unlocking the details of the assault against Taft graduate student Kirsten Wayborne. Yesterday, more of those locks tumbled and further details of the story came tumbling out as Negolian pursued his attempt at a plea deal by revealing more of his part in the murder plot. And today, as a result, Angela Shilliday is under house arrest in her home in Winchester, charged with solicitation to commit first degree murder. Once he began to open up, Negolian opened wide.

According to Negolian, Shilliday contacted him through "an associate" who arranged a meeting between the pair in a Cambridge Starbucks. Shilliday alledgedly explained to Negolian that Wayborne was "a threat" to her—a threat she wanted removed.

"I ast her what she wanted when she said 'removed'", Negolian is quoted as saying. "Like, did she mean murder? Assault? Just a bad scare? Each one of those things has a different price tag, ya know. Like, there's a sliding scale. She chose assault. That costs five large. Murder would have been ten grand."

According to Negolian, Shilliday acquiesced to his terms of $5,000 with $2,500 to be paid in cash to seal the deal and the remainder to be paid upon completion of the hit. Shilliday supplied him with Waybridge's name, a photograph from her Facebook page, her schedule at Taft University and her home address. She also advised Negolian that Waybridge traveled regularly to Boston on the Orange Line, passing through Downtown Crossing at the busy rush hour. She paid him $2,500 in hundred dollar bills to "remove the threat."

Negolian admitted that Shilliday did not enlarge upon her reasons for wanting "the threat [i.e. Wayborne] removed", nor did she mention Dr. Andrew Povitch, a winner of the Nobel Prize in Economics and a tenured professor at Taft University, who is rumored to be in an intimate relationship with Shilliday and recently with Ms. Wayborne as well.

Negolian "subcontracted" the hit to an associate, one Digger Diaz who, as has been previously reported—flubbed the assault, shoving Waybridge onto the MBTA tracks directly in front of an Orange Line train. The young woman was only saved from certain death only by the instant action of two passengers on the platform and the quick reflexes of the train operator.

Diaz was captured almost immediately by two other passengers, one of whom was an off-duty policeman.

"Diaz can't pick his nose correctly," Negolian said during his arraignment. "Diaz f—— it all up," Negolian complained. "Ah, I shoulda known he would."

Negolian is being held in jail pending his trial that is scheduled to follow the Shilliday trial. He is expected to testify in that case.

Nell put the paper down and sighed. This case was coming to a head just as Andrew's book was also approaching its climax. The manuscript was churning its way at a healthy pace through the publication process. Galleys were volleying back and forth between Rightmayer Press and the authors, and Nell felt like she was playing a doubles tennis match. She and Andrew on one side of the net and on the other side, the editor and publisher. It was happy work though—or would have been without the cloud of the Angela Shilliday case growing darker and darker on the horizon.

Chapter 44

At Taft University, in Winchester, and even in Nell's small cottage in Newburyport, Tish Penney's by-lined articles were being read with resignation and stoicism. But then the reporter breached the bounds of good taste and propriety by attempting to capture Andrew Povitch in her web of intrigue. Two articles, short though they were, attempted to draw the Nobel laureate into the scandal, and Madeline Kaiser was furious.

"This is supposed to be a reputable, metropolitan newspaper, not one of those muck-racking grocery store tabloids!" she fulminated. "Dragging Andy into this mess—*in print*—just isn't appropriate! D'you think he can sue for defamation of character?"

"Probably not," Nell said, "I think she hasn't actually crossed the line. Close to it though. Has Andy said anything?"

"Not much," Madeline conceded. "He's pretty closed-mouth these days. I know he's not happy though. It's a good thing Angela is under house arrest and can't show her face around the economics department. Andy isn't the only one who'd give her the cold shoulder."

Madeline Kaiser displayed a small, tight fist.

"Personally I'd like to give her more than a shoulder."

Nell changed the subject.

"The trial date is getting close. You're going to be a witness for the prosecution, I gather. Have you met with Kirsten's lawyer? Is he coaching you? Or how does that sort of preparation work?"

"Justin Doan is handling the case," Madeline replied. "Have you heard of him? His name is in the papers off and on and he's a very big deal at Twine and Brown, but he's quite unassuming actually. Very neat, buttoned-down guy. Soft-spoken. He feels the Waybornes' have a good case: solicitation of and conspiracy to commit first degree murder. The feeling is that Grenier will attack the murder assertion. Claim it wasn't murder because the victim survived. Doan thinks The Grinder will lean hard on Negolian's statement that Angela didn't want violence. Of course, Doan will point out that the outcome *would* have been murder without the interventions of outside influences, namely those two Good Samaritans who jumped onto the track and the sharp reflexes of the train driver. And without those interventions—which happened only by coincidence or fate—a murder is definitely what we'd be talking about. And speaking about talking, I don't think I should be. Anything I said, you didn't hear from me!"

"I shall have selective deafness," Nell declared solemnly. "I think I'd like to be in the courthouse for the trial. Don't ask me to explain why, I just want to be around."

Madeline shrugged. "Please yourself. You'll certainly know some of the players: Me. Andy will be summonsed, I imagine. And of course the lovely perpetra-tress herself—Angela."

Chapter 45

The caller introduced herself: Attorney Frances Marcucci, legal assistant to Attorney George Grenier. She continued, without missing a beat, to explain that they were in the discovery phase of Angela Shilliday's trial preparation and were interested in speaking with Nell. Would that be agreeable?

Nell indicated that it would. There probably wasn't a choice anyhow. Wouldn't they subpoena her if she said no? Hanging up, she wondered why lawyers were always so careful to attach titles to their names. Attorney This and Attorney That and John Doe, Esq. What if she were to demand a label also? Ghostwriter Nell Bane. Nell Bane, G.W.

"Yeah, right!" she scoffed aloud. "In a pig's eye."

But Attorney Frances Marcucci was willing to drive up to Newburyport for the interview—Nell was thankful for that—and she made sure to have cream on hand for the coffee. And a good thing too, for Frances Marcucci helped herself liberally to both cream and sugar. While she was busy adulterating her coffee, Nell took the opportunity to study the young woman.

Frances Marcucci was wearing a dark business suit, purchased off a rack in Macy's Nell guessed, without regard for the nicer details of tailoring that such a suit required. There was an unfortunate excess of material below the shoulders and the skirt needed to rise three inches to rescue it from dowdiness. Moreover, Attorney Marcucci's shoes had run-over heels. Feeling a stab of pity for the young woman, Nell smiled warmly in compensation.

"Now," she said. "How can I help you?"

Frances Marcucci produced a notebook and a small recorder.

"I'd like to record our conversation if you have no objection."

Nell did not, for these were the very tools of her own trade.

"In what capacity do you know Angela Shilliday?"

"Angela is—was, I guess—my client. She was writing a book—a biography—and decided to hire a ghostwriter to help her. I am a ghostwriter."

"This would be a biography of whom?"

"Dr. Andrew Povitch. He was awarded the Nobel Prize for Economics for his work in the field of ecological economics."

"And what is that exactly?"

Nell hesitated. "Do you really want me to go into it? It's quite complicated, and frankly, to the layperson, rather boring."

Frances Marcucci stared at Nell. Then must have decided she didn't want to be bored.

"We'll come back to that question."

Attorney Marcucci ate up the next ten minutes asking questions about the way Nell worked with Angela Shilliday. Then she came to the point.

"What Attorney Grenier and I are trying to establish," she said, "is whether you would be a suitable character witness to testify on behalf of Angela Shilliday. How do you feel about that? Would you have any hesitation? Might there be any reasons you feel you couldn't testify?"

Nell leaned back in her chair and looked pensive. Frances Marcucci watched her closely.

"I am going to be frank with you, Ms. Marcucci," she said. "I worked closely with Angela for about eight months, and the more I saw of her, the less I liked how she operated. I don't think she's an ethical person."

Frances Marcucci's jaw dropped. Her mouth didn't actually open, but Nell saw her jaw definitely drop. The young woman scrabbled to recover her professionalism.

"Would you care to elaborate?"

"I first became disturbed when she refused to let me interview Dr. Povitch for the book. That's when I discovered she intended to tell no one—especially Dr. Povitch—that she was receiving assistance with the project. That is her right, of course, but there's no shame in hiring a professional pen. One hires professional proofreaders and professional editors. Her secrecy was a red flag. Then I learned she had other secrets. For one, she intended for the book to do double duty. She was planning to sell it to the general market but also to use it as her doctoral thesis. If the book were her original work, that might be acceptable. However I feel strongly that a thesis should be the original work of the doctoral candidate and to hire someone to do it is less than ethical. Had I known about these issues at the start of our relationship, I would not have accepted the job."

Frances Marcucci was eyeing Nell coldly.

"Look," Nell elaborated, "this is just the way *I* feel. It isn't necessarily and universally unethical, but it does violate *my* code of ethics."

"So am I hearing you say that you won't testify as a character witness for Angela Shilliday?"

"I am saying that I *will* testify," Nell said firmly. "However I will speak my mind about my assessment of Angela Shilliday's character, and I have a feeling that what I have to say will not help your case."

Frances Marcucci switched off her recorder. She opened her briefcase and dropped her notebook and recorder into it. She shut the case with an editorial snap and stood up.

"I'm sorry you see it that way, Mrs. Bane," she said. Then she said something that a more seasoned lawyer probably wouldn't have said.

"I'm disappointed that you won't help your client—your *friend*. It seems that everybody's proving to be a false friend. We're having quite a bit of difficulty simply getting one or two people to speak up for Ms. Shilliday. If you change your mind—see your way clear to helping her—please give me a call."

Frances Marcucci placed her card on the table and saw herself out. Nell had the distinct feeling that Attorney Marcucci resented the time spent driving all the way up to Newburyport for nothing. Not even with a character witness to show for the trip.

Chapter 46

Nell was under the Boston Common once again. In the garage. This time, instead of walking south toward Madeline Kaiser's Bay Village condo or north to Robert and Jerry's perfect Beacon Hill townhouse, she headed east toward Pemberton Square and The Suffolk Superior Court for Criminal Justice. Despite its handsome architecture, the John Adams Courthouse—large, square and gray—was as dismal as a rainy day in February. Nell shivered.

She had no official business here since she had proven unworthy of standing as a character witness for the defense. She was simply drawn as a spectator to a scene of drama, and she didn't even know if she would be allowed into the courtroom. Still, she had an unaccountable need to be near the action. And so she allowed herself to be scrutinized by Security and finally given a pass to travel through the Great Hall where she goggled for a moment at the elaborately-decorated, arched ceiling before heading for the elevator. The fourteenth floor, she understood, was designated for criminal

THE GHOST WORKS A PUZZLE

business.

The corridor on the fourteenth floor was like an ant hill with people passing and re-passing, most of them hurrying and looking terribly, terribly busy. Those who weren't hurrying were idling on chairs along the walls. Waiting, and none too happily by the look of them. Nell found a vacant chair and located herself on it. She was waiting too—waiting to see what would happen next. It was going to be a long wait.

As time ticked on, Nell began to be able to identify some of the cast of characters. She could pick out the lawyers, striding along with briefcases, accompanied by their minions—various legal assistants who scurried with great stacks of paper and manila folders and serious expressions. The Wayborne family materialized. Anthony Wayborne broke away from the trio to speak to a colleague, but the woman whom Nell took to be Judge Catherine Lapp hurried her daughter into the courtroom. Now Justin Doan, Esq. joined the impromptu corridor conference. Nell studied him openly, knowing she would not be recognized. But when the Shilliday contingent arrived, she ducked her head. Tim Shilliday, along with Beth and his handsome younger sister Julia, walked briskly, looking neither left nor right. Julia Shilliday was wearing black again today, but this time it was a tailored pants suit with a white silk shirt and needle-heeled shoes that made Nell's toes throb just looking at them. Angela, she noted, was not with them.

Nell sat some more.

Madeline Kaiser and Andrew Povitch, walking side by side, passed her. Andy, barely turning his head, gave her a wink, and Madeline, looking straight ahead, allowed the side of her mouth to dimple in the familiar, elvish smirk but she did not slow her pace. Nell did not see anyone who might be Marky Negolian or, for that matter, Digger Diaz, but she supposed they would enter the courtroom through a special side door the way felons did in the crime shows she'd seen. She wondered if Angela would also be required to use this entrance.

Nell was sure that the rapacious Tish Penney was lurking somewhere nearby in a pack of media people.

The doors of the courtroom closed. Nell could hear no sound, and she knew the day would be long. She stood and stretched and strolled off in search of the ladies' room.

The court recessed for lunch. The re-opened doors released a rush of people intent on being first to the bathrooms, the vending machines, the places where cell phone use was permitted.

Nell also decided a breath of fresh air would be welcome and she wandered outside to stand in the shadow of the imposing but depressing courthouse building. However she was back in the corridor at one-thirty when the arguments in the case were rumored to be starting up again.

The corridor was quiet now and Nell found herself observing a woman she'd noticed earlier. She was tall and slender, slender to the point of thinness. She sat with her shoulders rounded and her legs drawn back under her chair; she was motionless except for her fingers which nibbled at each other continually. Feeling Nell's gaze, she looked up suddenly, startled.

Nell smiled.

The woman ducked her head shyly, then smiled too.

"Long day," Nell said, commiseratingly.

The woman swallowed and nodded in agreement.

"You're waiting for the trial in this courtroom?" Nell nodded toward the door closed on the Shilliday case.

"Yes. My sister ..."

"You're Angela Shilliday's sister!"

Nell was surprised for a moment, then realized how strong

was her resemblance to Angela. The distinction between them lay in their bearing. Angela's was proud and confident; this woman's affect was meek and self-effacing.

"I'm Nell Bane. I was working with your sister on a project."

Relief was apparent in the woman's face. What a curious emotion, Nell thought glancingly.

"I'm Judy Matusek," she said. "I'm here from Michigan because Angie wanted to have me here. Only," and here the woman dropped her eyes again, focusing on her picking fingers. "Only I couldn't stay in there—in that courtroom. It was just...too..."

She caught a breath that ended in a gasp.

Nell was on her feet and across to corridor to sit next to Judy Matusek. She placed her hand on both of Judy's. They were freezing.

"Listen," Nell said. "Let's get out of here for a short time. We're not going to know anything for a while. Let me buy you a cup of coffee. This must be very emotional for you. If I were in your position, I'd be a wreck. Come on."

And Judy Matusek from Michigan allowed herself to be led out of the Suffolk Superior Court for Criminal Justice.

Chapter 47

The High Spot Deli, despite its dive-sounding name, proved a good choice, Nell thought. She guided Judy Matusek to a quiet table, ordered two coffees and then convinced her companion to add an egg salad sandwich to the order. This took some persuasion, but Nell had perceived that a case of shredded nerves had kept Judy from eating any solid food that day, and in her opinion this was part of the reason the woman seemed so strung out. Over the rim of her coffee mug, Nell observed Judy Matusek carefully while pretending not to.

"Michigan is a lovely state," she said neutrally. "What part of it is home?"

"Not one of the lovelier parts, I'm afraid." Judy was apologetic. "We're from Flint."

"We?" Nell inquired. "Angela too? Flint is your hometown?"

'That's right. We all grew up there, the four of us. Bob, he's the oldest. I'm two years younger, then Angie came along three years after me, and Roger is the baby."

Nell allowed her silence and encouraging expression to stimulate Judy to share further. She was interested in learning more about Angela Shilliday from this new source.

Judy, picking up on the cues, continued. "Well, Dad was a paint salesman. Mom taught third grade. We certainly weren't wealthy, but we had a nice family life."

"Are your parents still living?"

"Mom died two years ago, and Dad's not well. Part of it is missing her, I guess, but he's got several health things going on—heart, diabetes. We haven't told him about Angie. He's so proud of her. Always has been. She was his pet—the star of the family. Our great success story. This would break his heart. Literally, I think."

Judy shook her head sadly.

"This thing has upset us all so badly. Bob's worried sick. He's worried about Dad and his own wife isn't well. And Roger's so disgusted with Angie that he stalks out of the room if her name is even mentioned."

Nell nodded sympathetically.

"He feels—Roger—that Angie had the best of everything. That she took everything, used up what she wanted, then threw the rest away."

"I'm not quite following you there."

"Well, to give you an example, my parents worked hard and saved to send us all to college. That was important to them. So Bob went off to Western Michigan and I followed him there two years later. But Angie wanted no part of Western Michigan. Or any state school, for that matter. She wanted to go to some fancy Eastern school, and she was adamant about it. She cried and argued and carried on for weeks."

Judy Matusek shook her head.

"I still remember it. We all do, I guess. Finally Dad said okay, that we'd manage somehow, and they took out a loan.

They'd never done that. They still had the fears from the Great Depression hanging over them, and they'd worked hard to save for our schooling, although we helped. Bob and I both worked in the dorms to help out. Well, Angie got her way finally and she went east to Taft. She loved Cambridge. Loved Boston. And to her credit, she worked too. It wasn't all take-take-take. But Roger was mad. When the time came for him to go to college, he went to a community college. He always said he didn't want to drive the parents deeper in debt, but he felt all the candy'd been sucked off the lollipop stick by the time he came along."

Judy Matusek looked unhappy.

"Then it came time for Angie to get married. Oh boy, that was another storm. I was married by then. Married Ronny Matusek in the Methodist church and our reception was in the church basement. In Fellowship Hall, with cookies and little sandwiches made by the ladies in Mom's Circle. We had a cake though. A beautiful cake from the best bakery. But Angie didn't want that. Didn't want the grand Shillidays from Winchester coming all the way to Flint to a reception in the church basement. She had the idea that she'd be married in Boston, and she couldn't understand why the parents didn't let her rent someplace nice. She insisted she'd handle all the details. They wouldn't have to do a thing. Except pay for it, of course."

Judy's smile was rueful.

"Well, that was an awful hard time. Mom and Dad hated to see Angie unhappy, but frankly, her plans were just too much for them. Then too, all their friends were in Flint, and all the relatives. They could hardly be expected to all traipse off to Boston for the ceremony. Then Dr. Shilliday—Tim's father—came to the rescue. He suggested that he and Dad should split the wedding cost and he offered to host the reception at their country club and have the ceremony in the family's church. In Winchester. And Tim was great too. He insisted that he just wanted a small wedding instead of a big blow-out. And he was finally able to talk Angie down to that. The affair was still a lot for the folks to swallow, but the Shillidays, to their credit, did their best to make the Johnson family comfortable. And Angie got her fashionable wedding. Not quite the fancy bash she'd hoped for, but she was smart enough to settle for half the loaf rather than none at all."

Bits of egg salad had spilled out of Judy's sandwich. Meditatively, she collected these with a moistened finger. Nell watched.

"Did you see much of Angela?" Nell asked finally. "Did she visit frequently?"

"No, not very much. Each of us made at least one trip east. Even Roger came once with Karen. And Angie and Tim seemed to enjoy showing us around Boston and the North Shore, but no, Angie didn't come home much."

Judy's eyes were still on her plate, but the egg bits were neatly collected at one side of the plate.

"And you're here now," Nell prompted. "Was that your sister's idea?"

"She said she needed someone in the courtroom who was in her corner. That was silly. The Shillidays have always presented a united front behind Angie. Probably for Tim's sake though, and Angie knows that Beth and Julia are really there to support him. And frankly, I feel bad for him too. Angie did some terrible things. I... well, I'm ashamed of her, and I just don't know what to say to any of them—especially to Beth who's always been so gracious. I feel like I don't deserve to sit with them. And when it came right down to it, I couldn't. The opening arguments started and the prosecuting attorney—Mr. Doan, is it? He said he planned to argue for conspiracy to commit murder and I started feeling like I couldn't breathe. Tim told me I was hyperventilating and to go sit in the hall. I never went back in."

There was more silence. Nell had allowed her coffee cup to be refilled and she continued to sip—or pretend to.

"Judy, I'm going to ask a hard question now. How do you think this terrible thing could have happened? How do you figure that Angela, the woman who seemed to have everything, didn't think she had enough? And why do you think she went to such extremes to get what she wanted?"

Judy Matusek gave Nell's questions some thought before she began to shape a slow answer.

"She always had to be the best, Angie. The smartest student. The top athlete. The prettiest girl at the prom. I remember once, this girl Janice Kaltenbach, she was elected president of the National Honor Society and Angie was furious. That was a plum *she* wanted. She craved it. And she insisted she was the one who deserved it. I think she said some pretty terrible things behind Janice Kaltenbach's back. But Angie wanted that NHS notch on her belt. She wanted it on her record. Angie was always thinking about her record. Her resume. She was working as hard as she could to pile up laurels that would help her get into Taft. But that wasn't the end of it though, Taft. She kept on pushing in college to be the best or the one in the spotlight, whatever the best was."

"And she married a physician," Nell continued. "A man with money and good looks and a position in an upper class town. With two absolutely beautiful and healthy daughters thrown in besides."

Judy Matusek took up the thread. "Yes and even that wasn't enough. She thought she needed a title too. Doctor Shilliday the economist. She needed to be recognized as an author."

"And," supplied Nell, "she needed to be loved by a man

who was even more famous and powerful than her husband—Andrew Povitch. She needed him to desire her."

Judy Matusek met Nell's eyes. She nodded glumly.

"Yes, all of that. All of that and more."

"We'd better head back." Nell shifted gears. "The court could be recessing anytime. Are you ready?"

Judy Matusek indicated she was.

Chapter 48

Andrew Povitch and Madeline Kaiser had their day in court, and they emerged from the courtroom with attitudes that reminded Nell of children let out of school for the summer. For both, it had been a day of tension and long silences and now, released and relieved, they were talking nine-to-the-dozen. Nell interrupted them long enough to suggest a celebratory drink—an idea that was instantly and loudly seconded by both—and the trio marched over to Bowdoin Street and strode into The 21st Amendment for a vodka martini (Povitch) and glasses of chardonnay (Madeline and Nell). Nell, like a spectator at a ping-pong match swiveled from one to the other as they shared impressions and observations, interrupting each other frequently.

Nell heard that Madeline's experience on the witness stand had been brief and non-contentious. She had simply responded to Justin Doan's questions as he attempted to establish Kirsten Wayborne's good character. Yes, Kirsten was a courteous and pleasant young woman who got on well with fellow students and professors. No, Madeline had never observed her to be devious, dishonest or meretricious. The defense had no questions for Madeline Kaiser.

"Well, they wouldn't, would they?" Madeline demanded of the other two. "Kirsten is the sympathetic character. The victim. If he tried eroding her character, it could only harm his case."

She regarded Nell and Povitch with satisfaction.

But Andrew Povitch had been more challenged. George Grenier demonstrated that his nickname "The Grinder" was well-earned as he grilled Povitch mercilessly about his relationships with Angela Shilliday and Kirsten Wayborne. Nell heard how Grenier had come at Povitch from every angle possible to get him to admit he'd enticed an innocent and married Angela into an illicit affair. That he had—Svengali-like—leveraged his power and position as a Nobel laureate to lure Angela—apparently a tender and vulnerable underling in his economics department—into a compromising situation. And then he'd dropped her! Broken her heart! And thus, broken-hearted, she had lost all sense of judgment and reality. Povitch, George Grenier as much as said, was a rapacious, serial Romeo. He had seduced Angela and enchanted her, had driven her almost insane with passion, then coldly left her

But here Madeline Kaiser broke in eagerly.

"He was no match for Andrew though!" she crowed. "Andy never lost his cool. He looked Grenier right in the eye and answered every question thoughtfully, and he was able to take on every single accusation and innuendo and turn it back at the lawyer. And in the end, it was Grenier who looked like the fool!"

She delivered a triumphant whack to Povitch's forearm. He gave a whoop of laughter as his martini sloshed and almost spilled.

"So what's Grenier's defense going to be?" Nell wondered. "What tack is he taking, can you tell?"

"I think it's clear that he will go after the murder part of the charge," Povitch answered thoughtfully. "The charge is conspiracy and solicitation to commit first degree murder— well, the solicitation part is pretty clear. Negolian may be a dodgy character but he has to be believed when he says that Angela contacted him—solicited his services. Even Angela admits to that, so it would be ridiculous to dispute it. But Kirsten Wayborne is very much alive and is sitting there in the courtroom, so there was no murder. And we know that Negolian is on record as saying that Angela specified she did not want "violent" action taken in the threat to Kirsten. When he got Negolian on the stand, Grenier hammered away endlessly on that point to make sure the jury heard it loud and clear. And when he got Angela on the stand he labored on and on about it some more."

"So Angela was called," Nell said. "How was she? Was she okay?"

"She was very controlled," Madeline answered thoughtfully. "Careful. Very slow to answer Doan's questions. She was under oath, of course, so she had to be truthful but she answered just as briefly as she possibly could. Gave no more information than she was pushed to give."

"Did she, by any chance, say how she'd gotten in touch with Negolian?" Nell asked. "That's a missing piece to this story that I just can't figure out."

"As it happens, yes," Madeline told her. "Under oath she had to admit to sending the emails to Kirsten and when those threats didn't work, she went looking for Negolian."

"But how?" Nell asked. "Where do you go to find a hit man? Storm windows, yes, I'd know how to find those. Order a pizza, sure. But how did she do it?"

"Very simple apparently. Six degrees of separation." Madeline grinned. "She started asking around Taft—very casually—and eventually found somebody who knew someone else and first thing you know, she has the name of Marky Negolian in her grubby little hand. They got together in a Starbucks someplace where they sealed the deal. She reported it all with a stone face. Made no apologies."

"It was painful to watch," Povitch said. "In fact, I couldn't watch. I just looked away into space and even tried not to listen."

A shadow crossed his face and he shook his head.

Nell changed the subject. She didn't want the holiday spirits dampened.

"So who else testified?" she wanted to know.

"Marky Negolian , of course," Madeline told her. "And the prosecution called a couple of character witnesses for Kirsten, including me. Doan also had a doctor from MGH describe Kirsten's injuries and her condition upon arrival at the hospital. And he had some questions for Andy."

Povitch took up the recitation.

"Yes, Justin Doan gave me the opportunity to be candid about the relationship with Angela, and I also had to be open about the relationship with Kirsten. That was difficult with her parents sitting twenty feet away. I'm not sure how much they'd known about us."

"Kirsten isn't a child," Nell told him. "She's in her mid-twenties and certainly entitled to carry on her own affairs. No pun intended."

Povitch smiled at Nell. "I appreciate that," he said simply.

"And what of Angela?" Nell wanted to know. "How was she? How did she act?"

Povitch and Madeline both considered this question.

"She was ... composed," Povitch offered. "Yes, that's how I'd put it. She sat at the table next to Doan and looked straight ahead. Very little expression."

"It was curious though," Madeline added slowly. "The Shilliday family was seated right behind the defense table, but she never looked around at them. Never smiled. Never acknowledged their presence. But did you notice this, Andy? Did you see how her fingers kept tap-tap-tapping on her leg? It was like she had an old-fashioned telegraph key and she just kept rapping away. That suggests she was really quite nervous."

Povitch's answer was a sad shake of his head.

"Did Grenier's team have any character witnesses for Angela?" Nell asked.

"A couple," Andrew Povitch said. "Just people who knew her socially though. No one who dealt with her professionally. No one from Taft."

"Well, certainly not!" Madeline exclaimed indignantly.

Povitch turned his martini glass, fished out the olive and popped it into his mouth thoughtfully.

"Another?" Nell pointed to the empty glass.

"I think not. It has been a day of awe and tension, and I want to go home and take a long, hot shower."

"And tomorrow?" Nell asked. "We'll all be back tomorrow. What happens then?"

"Closing arguments are about all that's left," Povitch told her. "Then it goes to the jury and we wait."

Madeline Kaiser yawned. "I'll have an early night, I think. At some point all this is going to crash in on me and I'd like to be in bed when it does."

Nell paid the bill and they said their goodbyes outside The 21st Amendment. The dinner crowd was not yet stirring in Boston, but the home-bound traffic would be thick on Storrow Drive and sluggish up Route 93 all the way to the 95 Junction. Nell discovered she too was tired.

But in the fridge at home, a treat waited— rhubarb soup. Made with the spring's early rhubarb, sweet and sour and pale pink— pink as dawn's first light.

RHUBARB SOUP

8 cups chopped rhubarb, approximately
4-1/2 cups chicken broth
1 cup granulated sugar
2 star anise
1/4 tsp nutmeg
Finish:
1-1/2 lemons
1/2 cup chicken stock
1 T + 1-1/2 tsp cornstarch

The day before, Nell had combined the rhubarb, 5 cups of chicken broth, sugar, cinnamon and nutmeg in a pot. This she'd brought to boil over medium heat, then reduced heat and simmered for 20 minutes or until rhubarb is soft. She'd strained the mixture and returned the liquid to the pot where she brought it to a low boil.

Next, off heat, she'd mixed the cornstarch and a half cup of stock, then added it slowly to the simmering stock, stirring until the mixture thickened slightly. She juiced the half lemon into the soup and chilled it. To serve, Nell would top the chilled soup with a dollop of Greek yogurt and a few grinds of white pepper.

Chapter 49

The adrenalin that had carried everyone through the first day of the trial ran dry by Day Two. Nell spotted Judy Matusek sitting alone, slumped in a chair in the corridor as she had been the day before. Sitting down next to Judy, Nell earned a wan smile when she asked, "How's it going?"

To herself she added, "I detest that question and now I've gone and landed somebody else with it."

Judy Matusek shrugged.

"Under the circumstances, I guess it's going as well as it could. Nobody said much at the house last night. Poor Tim looked exhausted and shut himself up in his study. With a bottle of Scotch, I think. Glorimar must have had a million questions but she was too tactful to ask them. I was dead dog tired myself and went off to bed early. Thanks again for that egg salad sandwich, by the way. It was the only sustenance I had yesterday."

"Well, this should be a shorter day," Nell said consolingly. "On the other hand, the emotional tension could be worse.

Depends on how fast the jury reacts to what they've heard."

Indeed, the courtroom doors opened just before noon and people filed out silently and decorously.

"It's in the jury's hands now," Beth Shilliday told Judy Matusek, adding, "Come along dear, we're going to stop somewhere for lunch before going home. Tim insists he's going to his office. I can't think what use he'll be."

Left to her own devices, Nell turned, as she so often did to her friend Robert Hutchins. She tapped his number into her cell phone and was told that yes, he was home to company. So Nell walked up the backside of Beacon Hill and down the more fashionable side toward Charles Street, zigzagging a bit to aim for Robert's street.

"I wasn't in the courtroom," she told Robert. "It just didn't seem appropriate and I don't even know if I would have been allowed in. I didn't ask. But I did want to be around, and I heard detailed reports from Andy and Madeline."

"How did the Waybornes seem?" Robert wanted to know.

Nell remembered that he and Anthony Wayborne were acquainted from their Harvard days and was able to report that all three Waybornes looked well and fit.

"So now you wait," Robert said.

"So now we wait."

"And what will you do while you wait?" Robert asked. "Your usual occupation?"

"Make soup you mean?"

"Yes," Robert smiled, "that's what I meant."

Nell stood and stretched.

"What a good idea," she said.

CREAMY SQUASH SOUP

2 tlb. unsalted butter
1 medium onion, finely chopped

2 stems of fresh rosemary

4 fresh sage leaves

2 lbs of butternut squash, peeled, seeded and cut into 2-inch cubes

2 medium Yukon Gold potatoes, peeled and cubed

3 cups chicken stock (plus more if needed)

2 cups water (plus more if needed)

Nell melted the butter in a medium saucepan, then added the onion and 1 teaspoon of salt. She cooked the onion, stirring it once in a while as she thought. Meanwhile, she tied up a little bag of herbs—rosemary and sage—and since she didn't have cheesecloth, she used a coffee filter. She added the stock and water, the potatoes and squash and finally the herb sachet to the pot and cooked the mixture until the vegetables were soft.

Nell fished out the herb sachet and discarded it. She let the soup cool a bit, then scrounged it with her immersion blender until it was creamy-smooth. A sprinkle of salt and some generous grinds of pepper finished it off.

Chapter 50

Nell wasn't present in The Suffolk Superior Court for Criminal Justice when the jury in the Angela Shilliday trial filed back into the courtroom. All she knew was what she heard from Madeline Kaiser and what she read later in Tish Penney's column.

Victim's Dad Pleads For Mercy
By Tish Penney

The jury in the trial of prominent Winchester socialite Angela Shilliday deliberated nine hours before returning a verdict of guilty of conspiracy to commit vicious assault. The original charge of conspiracy to commit murder was argued down fiercely by Shilliday's defense lawyer, Attorney George Grenier, in rebuttal to the closing argument of Justin Doan, Esq, attorney for the prosecution, who noted that a murder charge continues to hold even if the planned murder is aborted. The intention to murder continues to validate the charge, Doan insisted, even if the murder itself isn't carried out. The jury ultimately supported the defense's argument.

Sentencing is set for thirty days from this date, but a poignant victim impact statement is likely to impact the sentence that Judge Harold Levenger will set.

When it came time for victim impact statements, Kirsten Wayborne's father, Attorney Anthony Wayborne, of the Boston law firm Twine and Brown rose to address the court. Stating that he spoke for his daughter, who was the target of the assault, as well as for the victim's mother, Judge Catherine Lapp, Wayborne provided a moving plea for mercy in the sentencing of Angela Shilliday. Pointing out that he and Judge Lapp feel enormously fortunate to have their daughter with them, alive and well, they empathize with the pain the Shilliday family is enduring.

"We take the view that this unfortunate incident was an act of misguided passion that mistakenly got out of hand. Clouded by emotion, as her mind doubtlessly was, Ms. Shilliday failed to understand the implications of her actions. Under ordinary circumstances," Wayborne continued, "Ms. Shilliday would have had no association with an individual of Mr. Negolian's character. He and she were communicating on different levels; in other words there was serious miscommunication between them."

Concluding that the Wayborne family hopes that the Shilliday family can find peace and forgiveness among themselves, he noted that the Wayborne family respectfully asks for a minimum sentence for Ms. Shilliday so that she can return with all expediency to her family.

"Well, that's that," Madeline Kaiser summed it up. "It ended with more of a whimper than with a bang. And I hope that now we can all get back to business. I hope things will settle down in the economics department and that you and

Andrew can concentrate on his book."

Nell, agreeing, quietly hung up the phone. But even as she sat in contemplation next to the silenced phone, there was a rap at the back door. Bunty Whitney entered, knocking.

"You're home," she said.

"How very perceptive of you, Bunty."

Bunty ignored the mild sarcasm.

"I just read Penney's column. How do you feel about the verdict?"

"I'm still digesting it," Nell said slowly. "As Madeline Kaiser said just now on the phone, I too hope we can all get back to business. Back to normal."

"And what is that? Normal business?" Bunty wanted to know. "When have things ever been normal?"

Nell gathered her thoughts.

"Well, for Andrew, normal is primarily the book. His book is just about ready to make its debut," Nell said. "It's printed and published and the reviews will soon be showing up in the *New York Times* among other places."

"Then Andy will be hitting the road, I guess," Bunty observed. "He'll be on all the talk shows."

"Well, some of them anyway," Nell replied. "I don't really know how much media attention a biography of a Nobel laureate can be expected to attract. But we'll hope for the best."

"I would think," Bunty said mildly, "that the notoriety around the trial won't hurt book sales and media attention."

The two women sat side by side in silence, until Bunty poked further.

"What does it mean for the Shillidays?" she wondered aloud.

"I guess it means separation for a while," Nell said. "Even if she gets a light sentence, Angela will almost certainly be spending some time in a facility. What it means for the family—

for Tim and Angela—I can't begin to speculate. Any revelation of infidelity tests the bedrock of a marriage, but there's so much more to the Shillidays' situation than infidelity. *Whew!*"

Nell allowed the half-whistle to summarize the situation.

"You were right about Angela though," Nell said finally.

At a questioning look from Bunty, she continued.

"You said at the outset that she was a fascinating character—more interesting perhaps than the Nobel laureate himself. I couldn't really see it then. I thought she was more of a pest. I had a very illuminating conversation with her sister."

Now Nell turned to face Bunty.

"I took her to lunch. Made her eat a sandwich. She hadn't eaten all day. And while she was eating it I got her to talk about her sister while they were growing up."

And then Nell distilled for Bunty the details of Judy Matusek's revelations.

Bunty nodded.

"That sounds about right. It's all about Angela. She—Angela—has scarcity issues. You know, there's only so much to go around—only a finite amount of money, a finite amount of fame, a finite amount of sex appeal. If you have something, that means I can't have it. If you're in the spotlight, there isn't room for me."

When Nell didn't comment, Bunty continued.

"Angela," she declared, "has to be the bride at every wedding and the corpse at every funeral. Like Glenn Close in that movie—she's a real 'fatal attraction' character."

The two women allowed a second silence to set in while, each contemplated some interior music or theme. Bunty sighed finally, struck her knees with her hands and stood up.

"I'm meant to be filling an order for more coffee mugs, and my clay's drying out. I just wanted your reaction to the verdict. What will the sentence be, do you suppose?"

Nell shook her head wearily.

"I have no idea. None at all."

"Don't get up," Bunty directed. "I'll see myself out.

Chapter 51

Robert Hutchins had a surprise for Nell. He drove up to Newburyport to spring it.

"Do you know a publishing outfit called August Sommer?" he asked.

"Um," said Nell, trying to remember. She gave up. "No, I guess I don't."

"I shouldn't think you would," Robert said dryly.

Nell gave him a look.

"I have a nodding acquaintance with the august Mr. August Sommer. His publishing company specializes in sensationalism."

Here Robert paused to look tantalizingly at Nell.

She was annoyed.

"For Pete's sake, Robert, if you have something to tell me, spit it out! Don't go cozying around like a female character in *Gone With The Wind*. It doesn't become you."

Robert grinned.

"You came to Sommer's attention during the trial. All the

elements guaranteed to intrigue him were present: Nobel laureate involved in a love triangle, wronged woman takes out a contract on her rival's life, high profile families involved in a contentious trial, prestigious university connection, and as the cherry on the sundae, a credible writer is privy to all the steamy details."

"I'm not following this, Robert."

"In a nutshell, Nell, August Sommer wants you to write a book about this whole thing. Write it fast so they can get it on the market in thirty to forty-five days. Hard on the heels, in other words, of Povitch's biography. Sommer wants it sensational. Seamy. Juicy. And the money he'll pay is juicy too. Sommer found out I know you and asked me to introduce the proposal. He's champing to meet with you, of course, and to outline a more formal deal."

Nell frowned. She was confused.

"I don't think this is the kind of writing I do," she said slowly.

"It probably isn't," Robert agreed. "But I suggest you take twenty-four hours to mull it over. Consider it. It would be easy work since all the facts are fresh in your mind and the research has been done. You don't have another ghosting assignment lined up. And, as I mentioned, it could be lucrative."

"Huh," Nell said.

"And one more thing," added Robert, "you'd have your name on the book. This one wouldn't be ghosted. Of course, you might prefer to use a pen name—a pseudonym—given the sleazy reputation of the publisher and the value of your own good name.

"Dear God!"

That was Nell's final remark.

Chapter 52

Robert had said to take twenty-four hours to consider August Sommer's proposal. The best way to do heavy considering, Nell had always found, was to put the issue on a mental back burner while starting a kettle of soup on the Aga's front burner. Experience had taught her that when the soup was ready to ladle into a bowl, the issue had often resolved itself. She considered gazpacho, then decided against it. No, the situation demanded something that actually required cooking. Clam chowder would do. And she'd do it right, starting with fresh steamers instead of canned clams.

NEW ENGLAND CLAM CHOWDAH

Two quarts of steamers
1/4 lb of salt pork or slab bacon
1 medium onion, chopped
1-1/2 lbs of potatoes, chopped to bite-size
1-1/4 cups of bottled clam broth
1-1/4 cups of whole milk

2/3 cup of light cream or half-and-half
Pinch of dried thyme
Salt and pepper to taste

The chowder required a trip to the fish market for Essex clams and a detour on the way home into Fowle's Market for the bacon. Then Nell was ready to cook.

She steamed the clams, reserving the steaming liquid which she strained. She shucked the clams, chopped them coarsely and set them aside.

She cut the bacon into small chunks and fried them in a soup pot. When the bacon was golden brown, she removed the bits and squinted at the fat remaining in the pot. She'd need enough to cook the onions in, but not a whisper more, so she used paper toweling to blot out the hot fat until she judged that just the correct amount remained. In this fat, Nell gently cooked the onion until it was tender but not browned. She stirred in the clam liquid, broth, potatoes, milk and simmered it gently for about 20 minutes, never letting the liquid boil.

Just before serving, Nell added the cream, the clams and the seasonings, monitoring the chowder carefully so it wouldn't boil.

When the chowder was steaming nicely in a chowder mug, Nell sprinkled on the cooked bacon bits and a bit of minced parsley.

There were two schools of thought on chowder, Nell reckoned. Three, if you counted Manhattan clam chowder, but that was really below consideration. Tomatoes have their place, certainly, but not in chowder. But New Englanders either liked their chowder thick—thick enough to hold a spoon upright in the bowl—or those who properly appreciated the correct way— a chowder where the onions, potatoes and clams swim in in a broth made savory with the perfect amounts of milk, cream and clam liquid. Nell voted stoutly with the second group.

When she had reached the bottom of her chowder mug and wiped the mug clean, she pulled the August Sommer proposal into the forward part of her mind and went to her computer to write.

Chapter 53

Mr. August Sommer
August Sommer Publishing Co.
Columbus Ave.
Boston, MA

Dear Mr. Sommer:

Through our mutual acquaintance Robert Hutchins, I have learned of your interest in hiring me to write a book—or should I say an expose—of the recent trial of Angela Shilliday and the actions that precipitated that trial. I believe you know that Ms. Shilliday is a former client of mine and that she was contracted to write the authorized biography of Nobel laureate Dr. Andrew Povitch. When the work proved more than Ms. Shilliday could handle, she hired me to ghostwrite the book. Moreover, you must be aware of the relationship between Dr. Povitch and Ms. Shilliday as well as Ms. Shilliday's extraordinary actions that led to her trial. Finally, you must be know that Dr. Povitch asked me to complete his biography when Ms. Shilliday was no longer "in the picture".

All this is prelude. Now I'll come to the point.

I cannot accept your offer to write a book about the experiences I detailed above. The money you offer is tempting—that I will grant. But I do not believe it would be ethical for me to produce this sort of exposition. (I certainly can't call it literature.)

In my view, it would be unethical to prey upon the troubles of two already troubled families and of a gentleman who has made a splendid contribution to the field of economics. The Shillidays are a fine, upstanding family, dedicated to healing those in need of medical help. They are gentle and considerate people. Angela Shilliday's lapses in judgment were unfortunate, I'll grant that, but they do not give cause for further embarrassing her or the family. The Shillidays have suffered much and should now be left in peace. The same things can be said about the Wayborne family. I have no doubt they would be very disturbed by such a book as you propose.

Dr. Andrew Povitch's biography is coming out very soon, as I'm sure you know. I expect it to do very well on its own without the help—or should I say the confusion—caused by a sensationalist also-ran published by the August Sommer firm. There has been enough scandal. It's time to move on to more edifying matters.

In conclusion, Mr. Sommer, I thank you for your interest in me, but we shall not be working together.

Sincerely,
Eleanor Bane

Chapter 54

As Nell had predicted, Andrew Povitch was the subject of a number of interviews when the book, *The Economics of a Life: Andrew Povitch*, made its debut.

"It's like receiving the Noble prize all over again," Povitch marveled, "except on a smaller scale, of course."

"It's because you provide a good interview," Madeline Kaiser told him. "An interviewer only has to ask one question and you're good for twenty minutes. It's like dropping a quarter in a slot machine and—*ka-ching, ka-chang*—you're off to the races."

Povitch laughed. "Madeline, my darling, you know me too well. A prophet is without honor in his own country."

"And speaking of honor," Nell put in, "I'd like to honor you with a small party at my house. Just a few people and some good conversation."

"I accept!" cried Andrew Povitch. "I will get to see your little home in Newburyport at last."

Then Nell had an idea.

"Let's make it a Slovenian night! You know, in honor of the boy from Cleveland. Is there anyone from your hometown you'd like to invite Andy?"

"The only person I know who still lives in Cleveland is my first wife, Mira. And I don't think she'd accept the invitation. Although I would love to see her. No, invite whomever you wish Nell. I know they will be charming."

Chapter 55

And so Nell cast out invitations among her friends, offering the opportunity to meet the famous Nobel-winning Dr. Andrew Povitch and explaining that this book party would be a Slovenian celebration. Invitations were enthusiastically accepted and on this summer evening, the little house was party-ready, vibrating with the nervous energy of that half hour just before the first guests arrive—a backstage feeling of waiting for the curtain to rise. The evening air held an unseasonable chill so Nell had laid a small fire in the snug. Candles glowed, flowers spilled in profusion from every vase Nell owned, while in the backyard, saucer-sized blooms of white viburnum and hydrangea made their peculiar ghostly spotlights among dark leaves. Then at last came the celebratory sounds of arriving guests, each bearing a contribution to Slovenian Night.

Madeline Kaiser, revealing a hidden talent for baking, produced a remarkable *potica* that brought raves from all and the loudest acclaim from Andrew Povitch himself who pronounced it the best *potica* west of Slovenia and east of Cleveland. Bunty Whitney marched herself off to Fowle's Market and, in consultation with the butcher, bought eight pounds of the nearest thing to Slovenian sausages that a New England meat market could produce.

"What is a good Slovenian wine?" Jerry Gasso had asked when he and Robert were invited to the celebration. Then added, "Or is that a contradiction of terms? *Is* there a good Slovenian wine?"

But he and Robert Hutchins researched the subject and consulted with the owner of Charles Street Liquors and came bearing three bottles.

Jerry was triumphant.

"A sample from each region!" he crowed, introducing each bottle with a flourish. "Were you all aware that there are three wine regions in Slovenia?"

"*Voila!* A Cabernet Franc 2008 from Primorje!" he cried, revealing the bottle with a gesture worthy of a magician and setting it down with a plunk. "Next, a Gamay 2001 from Posavji!" *Plunk.* "And—from Podravje—a Rensiki Rizling 2011!"

"Ouch!" cried Andrew Povitch, clapping his hands over his ears. "You're mispronouncing outrageously! Stop! Stop immediately and bring me a corkscrew!"

Nell's great friends, the Fitzmaurices, brought a green salad brimming with vegetables from the local farm stands of Newbury and Newburyport. And Nell was finally able to try out the involved recipe for goveja juha—Solvenian beef broth—that she'd copied out when she was first researching Andrew Povitch's background.

Povitch was delighted with Nell's old friends Franklin and Ann Fitzmaurice.

"Ah ha!" he said to Franklin, "so you teach at B.U. We are

colleagues then. Just at different institutions. Tell me, how many classes a week do you handle? And seminars, do you find those delightful?"

And Povitch and Franklin were off for a jovial occupational conversation that finally had to be broken up by Madeline Kaiser.

Andrew Povitch refreshed his glass of wine and held his glass high.

"It is the custom in Solvenia," he announced, "to greet friends at mealtime with these words—simple and sincere— *Dober Tek*! Good appetite to you! And so to you, good friends— old and new—*Dober Tek*!"

The guests wandered into the garden, sipping Slovenian wine and a remarkable beer that Nell had discovered. All agreed that the goveja juha delivered the promised energy and appetite for the rest of the meal. And as the evening wound down, the last of the wine consumed and every crumb of *potica* licked up, everyone settled in the snug to reflect and watch the fire burn down to embers.

"All's well that ends well." Jerry Gasso offered a clichéd benediction.

Andrew Povitch took mild issue.

"For some of us it ended well. I have my authorized biography at last. Young Kirsten Wayborne escaped irreparable harm and is finally well and headed to Portugal for a six-week vacation. Madeline is returning to Ohio to collect her sister so they can fly off to cruise the fjords of Norway. Our Nell here, having turned down the opportunity to exploit me and the long-suffering Shilliday family in a scandalous expose, is on sabbatical from writing assignments. So for us, the events of these last months are ending well. The exception—or one exception anyway—is Angela."

Silence settled like ash on the group. Then Robert

Hutchins spoke softly.

"Please tell us, Andrew, what you can about her sentence."

Andrew Povitch cleared his throat.

"Anthony Wayboune's victim impact statement made quite a difference in Angela's outcome, I believe. She was given eighteen months in the Women's Correctional Facility in Framingham to be followed by a program of community service, close monitoring by a court-appointed social worker and regular counseling by a psychologist. Of course, there was a fine as well. $5,000. For the crime of which she was accused, that seems a lenient sentence indeed."

Robert Hutchins nodded.

"It was generous of the Waybornes to see it that way," he observed.

"They had their day in court," Povitch agreed, "but they didn't insist on a pound of flesh."

He rubbed his chin and considered further.

"Mr. Negolian bought himself a measure of latitude by bringing forward his testimony against Angela, but he too is due to spend several seasons in the slammer."

His own slang term made Andrew Povitch grin.

"Negolian's accomplice, Mr. Diaz, is also incarcerated, however that is not new to him, I understand. For him, jail is a sort of homecoming. I don't believe he will be working further with Negolian however."

There was more silence as the group individually mused on the impact of these sentences, but Bunty Whitney at last spoke the question nobody wanted to ask.

"What about the Shillidays' marriage? Will Dr. Shilliday ask for a divorce, d'you think? Or is he likely to forgive his wife and welcome her back?"

Silence again. Finally Nell decided this was her territory.

"I keep in occasional touch with Glorimar Jones, the

Shillidays' nanny-housekeeper. She's been keeping the place afloat for months now, helped out by Beth Shilliday, Tim's mother. Glorimar is sensible and calm and has been a rock for those little girls. But it has been difficult. The girls know some things are very wrong but they don't quite understand what. Mummy's in trouble and when they see her, she is not the Mummy they knew. Daddy's different too. Remote. Sad. That big house is awfully quiet. Glorimar claims not to have an opinion on the outcome of the Shillidays' marriage. Tim may forgive Angela or he may not. He may buy into Angela's remorse—if she turns out to have any. Maybe they'll stay together for the girls' sakes, maybe they won't."

Nell paused, but no one commented, so she continued.

"Judy Matusek—that's Angela's sister who came out from Michigan for the trial—has gone home, and I've wondered if Angela's family back in Flint has forgiven her. I wonder if they ever told the father that his fairy tale princess turned out to be the story's wicked witch. I doubt I'll ever know."

Nell, perhaps more than people who were not writers and who did not have to craft endings, understood that not all stories are happily-ever-afters.

"Some stories have happy endings," she said, picking up on Jerry Gasso's comment. "Others don't. And there are some stories whose endings we never know. Endings that continue to puzzle us. Cause us to continually ask why. And they can be very intriguing stories indeed. Stories to which we keep returning and trying to puzzle out. Perhaps Angela Shilliday's story is one of these. But I do believe in the human power to heal. Kirsten Wayborne's lovely young body gives testament to that. The human psyche, if it heals, isn't as easy to see as a physical recovery, but it is my hope that Angela will heal. I hope that she—whether her marriage is intact or whether it's broken—will find peace. I hope we all do."

∼

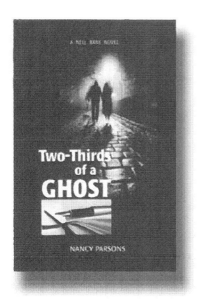

Two-Thirds
of a
GHOST

A Nell Bane Novel

Nell Bane is a ghostwriter. When she begins to suspect her high-powered and high-minded client David Kernow isn't quite who he presents himself to be, she begins to unwind his story and finds that her ethics—and possibly her life—are in jeopardy. Ethics, psychology and intrigue are the hallmarks of a Nell Bane novel. As the ghostwriter delves into her clients' stories, she is drawn deeper into their lives.

> This first book in the Nell Bane series introduces the ghostwriter and a small cast of "supporting players" who will appear in subsequent books; each book in the series introduces a new client for the ghostwriter and a new set of characters and plots guaranteed to build suspense and keep the reader turning pages.

Order the Nell Bane series from the publisher's website.
www.cheshirepress.com/books_fiction.html
or from Amazon.com or from your favorite bookstore.

Made in the USA
Lexington, KY
09 July 2014